THE
GORGON
FESTIVAL

Also by John Boyd

THE
GORGON
FESTIVAL

by
John Boyd

WILDSIDE PRESS

For Leesa and Jennifer Le Doux

CHAPTER ONE

As a youth Alexander Ward had escaped from poverty into violence when he went from the Depression into World War II, and he had returned from the ruins of Hitler's Reich accepting as his credo a remembered fragment from a medieval manuscript, "Because I did not lyke to fyte and wanted to rede, I went into the monasterie."

Since there were no monasteries for free-thinkers, Ward entered the academic world and found even there, on administrative levels, competition and conflict. So he concentrated on teaching and research in molecular biology until the Student Rebellion reached Stanford. Then he retreated to the innermost cloister of scholarship, pure research.

Now, on a Friday afternoon in late May, he walked up the steps of his Palo Alto home feeling uneasily triumphant over a discovery that would probably earn him a Nobel Prize and bring the world into his cloister, unless he were ejected from the cell beforehand for non-payment of his academic fief. Ward had not published in a learned journal in three years.

Ester was approaching from the stepped-down dining room as he entered. As always, she walked in beauty, but there was petulance in her voice.

"Alex, you're late. The caterers are here, Doctor Carrick's on his way, and you haven't shaved."

It was also the day of the last faculty cocktail party of the semester, he remembered.

"I had photography to finish at the lab," he explained. "Today I added some missing rungs to a DNA ladder and the molecule replicated itself. I've created life in a test tube."

1

"That's wonderful, but Carrick sent over only two bottles of vodka. If we run short, the guests will blame me."

Ward was not crushed by her reaction. Had he been Champollion announcing translation of the Rosetta Stone, he knew she might have merely asked, "What did it say?"

It was not that Ester was unintelligent, it was merely that her area of specialization differed from his. Twelve years his junior, she had been his lab assistant until he married her to break the production bottleneck her presence in his working area created.

"Don't worry, dear," he said, bending to kiss her. "Guests at faculty cocktail parties rarely drink vodka."

What a beautiful face, he thought as their lips touched; a pity no one ever noticed it, but understandable. Not until the third day of their honeymoon had he discovered she had green eyes.

"Ruth Gordon guzzles it," she contradicted. "Besides, I've invited a gentleman from San Francisco who has to drink vodka."

"Don't worry about us peasants. Concentrate your charms on Carrick. If you can get him to extend my research grant, I'll take you to Stockholm for your day's work."

He started up the stairs but, remembering, he stopped halfway to the landing and looked down at her. "Ester, there's a fifth of vodka in my private stock if your policeman friend needs it."

She slapped her hands to her hips and looked up at him in admiration mixed with exasperation. "Just how did you know Joe Cabroni was a policeman?"

In the fishnet cocktail dress she had picked up in Monterey during her fisherman period, above a waist so narrow he feared for her digestion, Ester's torso was bifurcated by cleavage unequaled west of the Grand Canyon. She wore no brassiere, but her see-through dress had strategic triangles woven into the netting. Her breasts reminded him of the heads of two jewfish trying to batter out of a seine.

"If they have to drink vodka and it isn't lunch time, you don't figure them for bank tellers," he said, and turned back up the stairs.

Actually he had been given stronger clues to Ester's policeman period by her shopping trips to San Francisco; she was buying heavily in tailored blue outfits. But he was not concerned by his wife's excursions. She was intensely loyal and he valued loyalty above fidelity, which he considered no more than canine expediency.

Besides, he was aware of his own deficiencies.

Once a fortnight was his connubial limit, and then he had to prime himself, at times, by peeking at certain paintings in his art folios. By the time he reached retirement age he might have to resort to hard-core pornography, but he doubted that every other Tuesday would ever become an evening reserved for Parcheesi.

Ward laid the before-and-after electron microscope photographs of the DNA he planned to show Ruth Gordon in his shirt drawer, undressed, and went into the shower. With Ruth he could make no claims to brilliance with his discovery, for his use of electrolysis as a bonding agent had been guesswork and he knew of no reason why an electric current should bring about molecular linkage.

He stepped from the shower to shave and practiced a smile in the mirror for Doctor P. Frederick Carrick, N.P. The N.P. stood for the Nobel Prize which Carrick shared with a biologist at Osaka University for discoveries relating to testerone, and in this instance the initials were mildly pejorative. Carrick was an academic equivalent of a Texas oil man. He wore a vest in order to carry an old-fashioned watch because he needed the watch fob to display his Phi Beta Kappa key, and his money came from a family-owned pharmaceutical house. As head of the biology department, he okayed all requests for government research grants and acted as host at department cocktail parties.

A bachelor, he had enlisted Ester's aid at such parties as hostess, an arrangement which suited her and did not displease Ward, particularly now that Carrick had been making oblique remarks about his difficulties with grant extensions. Ester had Lady Macbeth's flair for politics and she might have gone far had she been married to Macbeth.

Voices were already rising from below when Ward descended the stairway, but he did not feel remiss about his tardiness. He was official greeter for Ruth Gordon only, and she was not due for another six minutes, precisely.

Ruth Gordon was rigid about schedules. Since God was dead and all morality relative, she had told Ward, she used the clock as a guide to conduct. Horological ethics were Ruth's answer to the decay of morality.

Carrick was standing at the entrance with Ester, telling her of his visit to Soho during a recent biology conference in London. Ward crossed the living room, smiling, and extended his hand in greeting.

"Hello, Alex," Carrick's voice boomed for all to hear. "Where've you been? Upstairs writing a paper for publication, I trust."

Instead of shaking Ward's hand, Carrick put his empty glass in it and said, "One double bourbon, boy."

Carrick's pratfall humor had an edge, Ward knew, as he turned toward the bar with the glass. The department head was preparing him for a rejection of his request for a grant extension on the basis that his experiments were not being shared with the scientific community.

By the time Ward returned with the drink, Ruth Gordon was honking for him to come and move his VW, with which he blocked the drive when Ruth was coming to assure her a parking place.

Ward walked out, waved to the woman in her old Chevrolet, and began to push his car forward, calling back to her, "Weak battery."

After he had pushed his car into the carport, he rushed back to assist Ruth, but she was slamming the door behind her and standing erectly outside the car without the aid of a cane.

At seventy, Ruth Gordon was still handsome, firm featured, clear-eyed, her steel-gray hair beautifully groomed. Smiling she swung toward him with military crispness caused by her arthritic spine.

"Alex, your antic steps tell me you're excited. Another of your theories, no doubt. Did I see Carrick and your other half at the door? Well, get me past Narcissus and the Earth Mother quickly. I have two hours and twenty-three minutes allotted for freeloading."

Smiling, Ward took her arm. With the arrival of Doctor Ruth Gordon, professor emeritus of gerontology, his boyhood friend and mentor, widow of his old headmaster, the party had begun for Ward.

Shadowed from the westering sun by a wisteria arbor, Ward sat with Ruth, a vacuum flask of vodka and orange juice on the patio table in front of them, sipping and listening to fragments of conversation from the patio. Four years ago, before she developed arthritis, Ruth had been a teetotaler. Her doctor had suggested a glass of wine at bedtime to aid her circulation, and when arthritis hit her, she increased the dosage to a fifth of vodka a day.

Beyond their bower, bits and pieces of gossip drifted to them. With the silence of long friendship, they listened.

"The filter separates the nuclei from the ribosome like whey from clabber . . . Did you get an eyeful of those breasts? No wonder Ward never publishes . . . Did you read Carswell's paper on catalyst for amino linkage? Sound waves, and he tries to foist the idea off as original . . . He doesn't have to publish. A pair like that's worth six papers a year . . . I used a C-note tuning fork as an undergraduate . . . Ward should sell shares . . . Henderson asked for eighty thousand but Carrick cut his request to twenty grand."

Ward never talked shop with other biologists, because he never knew when his listener might grab an idea and run with it.

"Donne is undone," he commented to Ruth with a wave of his hand toward the guests in the patio. "Each man is an island entire of itself."

"One more reason to keep open lines of communication

with the young," she said. "I've given up on intervening generations."

"How are you coming with your youth movement?"

"Continuing the dialogue," she said, with obvious satisfaction. "Tomorrow I lecture on roses to the San Jose Teen Horticulturists Club."

"The anti-grass lecture?"

"Yes, and Sunday, at the Beethoven, Brahms, and Bach luncheon, to guests from Palo Alto High School. My anti-rock lecture."

"Continue your dialogue, Ruth, but stay on the rostrum. Don't get down among them."

"You don't talk down to today's youth," she flared. "They detest pomposity."

Ruth was prickly in certain areas and Ward diverted her. "Speaking of pomposity, Carrick sounds as if he doesn't intend to extend my research grant unless I publish, so I'm planning a paper to be read before the national convention."

"That's why you came skipping out to greet me. What have you done that's worth a paper?"

"Reconstituted a fragmented DNA molecule from the ribosome of a muscle cell and observed its replication."

He took the photographs from his pocket and handed them to her casually, figuring any onlooker outside the arbor would assume they were family snapshots.

"For your eyes only," he said. "Before and after."

She cupped the photographs in her hands and shuffled slowly through them. To an inexpert eye the DNA molecule resembled gray intertwined beads immersed in ashes, but Ruth grasped their importance at once. Her interest was so intense her expression seemed furtive.

"Have you translated the code of the replicated molecule?"

Ward shook his head. "I haven't had time. Rungs in the ladder were supplied by a complex molecule of sugar phosphate I'll describe in my paper, so the reconstituted DNA should not differ from the original."

"I'll decode from the photographs over the weekend," she said.

If she had asked his permission to decode the DNA molecule, he would have refused in order to spare her feelings. The ribosome was from the muscle cells of a hamster, and Ruth was a woman with odd passions; schedules, roses, classical music, young people, and hamsters.

"How did you create the linkage?" She asked.

"Electrolysis," he answered. "But I don't know why. I was just playing around."

"Don't publish a single word, Alex, until you analyze the reaction. Why? Because Nobel Prizes aren't awarded for happy accidents. Have you thought of practical applications of the discovery?"

"Casually," he had to admit. "Such bonding in chromatin might prevent sickle cell anemia, haemophilia, or Mongoloid births. If it could be introduced into human body cells it might cure cancer."

"That's bush league, boy!" Her whisper was a snort of disgust. "Are you telling me you've never heard of the theory of random error . . ."

"Hide your French postcards, Ruth." Ester's voice, husky with an overload of hormones, sounded above their table. "I have a member of the San Francisco vice squad with me . . . Detective Lieutenant Joe Cabroni, Doctor Ruth Gordon, a specialist in old age, and my husband, Doctor Alexander Ward, her once and present student."

Joe Cabroni's lips smiled as he took the hand Ruth extended, but his eyes were cold. Ward rose to greet a man wearing the ringlets of Apollo above the face of Adonis atop the body of Hercules.

"Actually," Cabroni said, "I'm with homicide."

"Stay away from the vice squad, young man," Ruth said. "Vice makes a man immoral."

"Pleased to meet you, Joe," Ward said, putting his hand into a mangle. "I rather expected a sergeant. Now I know where I can get my traffic tickets fixed."

"I don't handle traffic, but if you murder anyone, see me."

"Isn't he handsome, Alex?" Ester asked.

"Handsome and formidable. Welcome to the party, Joe, but don't get too drunk to drive."

"No sweat," Cabroni said. "I know a man who can fix traffic tickets."

As Ester ushered him away to meet other guests, Ward saw Cabroni's face set in anger as he glanced down at her, and the policeman's hostility alarmed Ward. Ester might find it harder to drop him than her poet, fisherman, interior decorator, et al.

"I didn't like that man's eyes," Ruth commented and turned back to Ward. "Have you told anyone else about this discovery?"

"I tried to tell Ester, but what's this about random errors?"

"Tell no one. You may have a cure for arthritis, and if Carrick found out, you'd never get your grant extended without giving his pharmaceutical company a piece of the action . . . How long will it take to find a theory to explain your facts?"

Ward shrugged. "Probably longer than I keep the lab, if I don't publish."

"When can you come to my house in absolute secrecy?"

"Tomorrow. Ester should be away on an overnight shopping tour to San Francisco."

"Listen carefully." She leaned closer. "Come up at 7:33 tomorrow evening. Bring a pint of solution and your electrolysis equipment. I've got an absorbent I use on my arthritis which should carry the solution to internal body cells, and I have an arthritic hamster we can use for the experiment . . . Now, Alex, you get right up from this table, corner Carrick, and demand an extension of your research grant. Tell him you're working on a secret formula for an aphrodisiac—that'll stop him—and the research is too personal to publish."

Ward sought Ester first and found her near the bar talking to five young graduate student instructors who were jostling for a front view. As he went by her to the bar, he gave her elbow a conspiratorial touch and shouldered his way through to order a double Scotch. It was best to be anesthetized when one cornered Carrick.

Ester joined him and leaned backward against the bar, whispering, "What's up?"

"I'm cornering Carrick. Get him alone for me. If I run into trouble, I'll report later. Where's Cabroni?"

"He was miffed because he thought I squealed on him to you . . . Double bourbon, bartender . . . To make him suffer, I introduced him to some New Leftists who are roasting the pig."

"After you isolate Carrick, rescue Cabroni," he said, alarmed by her cavalier treatment of the primitive.

They sighted Carrick in the living room talking to a visiting professor from Cambridge whose name evaded Ward but who, he remembered, had been knighted by Queen Elizabeth for his work in the mathematics of molecular structures. The Englishman was deferred to on the campus because most of Ward's colleagues didn't know a knight from a lord and considered him nobility.

"I'll peel off the limey," Ester said, "and you give Fred this drink."

She handed Ward the double bourbon and moved ahead of him with a more pronounced sway to her hips than usual.

"I say, Sir Doctor Peter Waverly-Pritchard, old chap, are you having a love affair with this bloody Yank, Carrick?"

"We've just had a falling out," Waverly-Pritchard smiled.

"You need fresh gin and tonic, and I want to introduce you to an elderly lady who's friend of a friend of yours, Queen Elizabeth."

She had the Englishman by the arm, leading him away, and her otherwise masterful ploy, Ward thought, was marred by a touch of malice. Indeed Ruth Gordon had been presented to the Court of St. James's, but Ruth preferred to drink alone, as Ester well knew.

"Enjoying your party, Fred?"

"I was, Alex." Carrick looked down at his empty glass.

"Presto," Ward said and produced the drink from behind his back. "Now I've patted your back, you pat mine. Sign my extension request."

"I'm taking it under advisement," Carrick said.

Since no one advised Carrick, and since his signature, as a Nobel scientist, was tantamount 'to government approval of Ward's research grant, Ward could only read Carrick's remark one way.

"Fred, I take this as a vote of no confidence in my research project."

"Alex, I have confidence in your work, on the gut level."

"How do you acquire confidence in a complex biologic experiment on a gut level?" Ward asked.

"Well," Carrick was hesitant, "married to Ester, you wouldn't spend so much time in your laboratory if the work wasn't important, but nobody knows what you're doing out there in the annex. You never publish your findings."

Here was the spot to introduce Ruth's tactics, but Ward had spotted a fallacy in Ruth's suggestion. If Carrick wanted a piece of the commercial action in a cure for arthritis, he'd want four-fifths of the play in an aphrodisiac.

"But you have confidence on the gut level," Ward reminded him.

"True, but there's another consideration, the paucity of your request. You're asking $22,000 for a two-year grant. That sum won't impress the Federal boys, and Stanford is a proud university. It monkeyfies our image to ask for peanuts. Since no one knows what you're doing, the only way to impress the government with the importance of your work is by the size of the grant. I advise you to up your request to $180,000."

"Fred, I'm not building a cyclotron."

"The government doesn't know it."

"What could I do with $180,000?"

"This research business being what it is," Carrick said, "we have to take care of our better graduate students. I have eight good boys with no place to go. If you would consider adding them to your staff, the grant might be extended."

Suddenly Ward remembered a fragment of patio gossip, "Henderson asked for eighty thousand, but Carrick cut his request to twenty grand."

Things were adding up. Carrick wanted to put spies in his laboratory. If Ruth was correct, if he had discovered a cure for arthritis, the adroit pragmatist, Carrick, would have the product past the Pure Food and Drug Administration and onto the market before Ward could formulate an analysis of the DNA bonding process.

"What's your deadline for extension requests?" Ward asked.

"July thirty-first."

Little more than two months remained for Ward to find the answers, and he didn't yet know the questions. Finding out would cut into his Tuesdays with Ester unless Ester, herself, could pull a coup.

Returning to the patio, Ward saw Ester standing beside Cabroni. Around the police lieutenant, gesticulating guests were hurling words against Cabroni's granite face.

As Ward neared the group, he heard someone say, "The fallacy of the police mentality lies in its tacit assumption of the father role."

"I deny paternity charges," Cabroni answered. "The bastards are not of my making."

Cabroni was handling the dialectics, all right, Ward decided as he moved up beside Ester and said, "Carrick's giving me a qualified 'No.' He wants me to publish or work with a staff. Either way, he figures to find out what I'm doing."

"Guard Cabroni's flank," Ester said, "and I'll try my hand with Carrick."

Ward decided on a diversion. Turning, he tapped Cabroni's shoulder.

"Joe, I'd like to make a statement. To me, the initials P-I-G stand for pride, integrity, guts. In the continuing dialogue with youth, certain concepts must be stressed, and nothing stresses a concept so much as a billy club . . ."

Moving away, Ester sensed her husband's political tactics and applauded him. Alex was diverting the anti-police bias of the group by offering himself as a sacrificial goat. Ester was proud of her husband and delighted by the image of Alex as a goat.

When excited, Alex had the most sensual walk in the world. On his blunt-toed feet extended from long legs swung slightly forward on his pelvis, he pranced toward her like the front half of a goat pulling a cart on every other Tuesday, and Ester always tingled when he walked.

Carrick stood near the bar with another professor talking of nucleotides. Ester caught his eye and pointed toward the front door with a swing of her shoulders. Without a word, she walked through the living room and onto the front porch. Shortly thereafter, Carrick stood behind her.

"I know you're interested in horticulture, Fred, and I wanted to show you my geraniums."

Carrick had no interest in horticulture, but he was gallant. "Ester, I've always wanted to take a good peek at your geraniums."

She took him by the hand and led him to the steps, where they paused. She took a single step down from Carrick and turned toward one of the boxes flanking the steps on concrete abutments. The geraniums flared pink in the sunset.

"Aren't they gorgeous, Fred?" she said, looking down at the flowers.

"Never saw anything like them before," Carrick agreed.

"I wish you could see them in broad daylight."

"Ester, they'd be beautiful at night, *especially* at night."

She averted her eyes to the flowers to let Carrick peek unseen. Academic men were shy and she had a technique, Alex called it antiphrasis, which she used on shy men.

"Fred, you're a handsome, impressive man with your lion's mane hair and your Phi Beta Kappa key dangling.

Do you ever think of taking time off from your grubby old office?"

"Some times more than other times, but I'm an administrator with a staff that's more willing than able, and it's hard to keep my staff on an even keel." His voice trailed off.

From years of practice, Ester had learned to read a man's conversation on a subliminal level. Carrick had a mild case of impotency, she decided.

"You might find someone who could handle it for you. Perhaps a woman. Some women have capacity you men never suspect."

"I've got all kinds of problems," he said.

"I specialize in problems."

"Some are confidential."

"I can keep a confidence."

"Even from Alex?"

"Especially from Alex. Why don't you drop by Wednesday for lunch? That's the maid's day off and Alex always takes lunch in his laboratory. We can discuss our problems."

"Do *you* have problems, Ester?"

"Alex is my greatest problem. He's at the laboratory so much of the time; there's no staff to take care of things."

"Why does he like to work alone?"

"He says other people's world lines warp his world lines and he can't concentrate."

"What's he doing down there in the annex, anyway?" Carrick's voice sounded peevish.

Out of loyalty, Ester never spoke of Ward's work, knowing his love of secrecy. "Carpentry work," she evaded. "He is putting rungs back in broken ladders."

"Fixing ladders, eh? Warped world lines? Maybe Alex has a problem . . . Well, I'd certainly like to meet you Wednesday."

Nervously, Carrick clinched and unclinched his hand. "You do that, Fred. I might help you firm up some of your weak areas, realign your staff."

Ester looked away, inwardly troubled. She had been careful not to operate on campus. Some men were indiscreet, and she didn't want Alex's colleagues to think she was married to a cuckold. But Alex wanted the Nobel Prize, and there was no sacrifice she wouldn't make for her husband.

"I swear, Ester," Carrick breathed above her, "you have the most beautiful geraniums in the world."

"Somebody wants you, Doctor Carrick," Joe Cabroni called from the doorway, "way back in the rear of the patio."

"I'll see you later, Ester, and thanks for showing them to me."

Cabroni was obviously angry as he walked up.

"What did he mean by 'I'll see you later'?"

"At the buffet table, Joe. It's almost time to be served."

"What were you showing him?"

"My geraniums," she pointed to the flower box. "Has someone given you a bad time, Joe?"

"Not me, but your husband's about to get lynched while you're out here flirting with that geranium-loving pansy."

"Are you telling me the barrel-chested Doctor Carrick is a pansy?"

"That's no barrel chest. That's his bosoms. We learn a lot about perverts down at headquarters and believe me, Ester, he's a morphadyke."

She would have to ask Alex what a morphadyke was, she thought, as she took Cabroni's arm and steered him back toward the house. Fifteen years with Alex had aroused in her a bemused curiosity as well as an awareness of inconsistencies in logic.

"Should you fear for my virtue around a pansy, Joe?"

"He's got fingers," Cabroni muttered. "I could tell by the way he kept moving his fingers, his female half's a Lesbian."

Ester's duties as a hostess kept her from reporting to Ward immediately, but after she started the guests on the buffet, she managed a word with him.

"I don't know where we stand with Carrick, yet. Joe got jealous and broke up our conversation. Joe says Carrick's a morphadyke."

"The word is 'hermaphrodite,'" Ward told her. "It means one who is half a man and half a woman."

"That would make for a cozy arrangement." Ester spoke lightly, but she was troubled. With only half a man to work with, and that half impotent, she had a problem with Carrick.

CHAPTER TWO

Late Saturday afternoon under jacarandas arching purple over Pinyon Verde Lane, Ward nursed his VW up the hill to Ruth Gordon's house, but he was less concerned about weak car batteries than about yesterday's conversation with Ruth. She planned to use only one hamster for the experiment.

Although in later years she had grown crochety and frank in speech, Ward had never suspected Ruth of mental disintegration even when she turned her experimental animals into pets, and he considered multiple pets the last infirmity of a failing sentimentalist. Yet, however devoted to hamsters she might be, as a scientist she should know one animal did not constitute a control group.

High above Palo Alto, in a modified Gothic house flanked by groves of pines, Ruth lived in such isolation Ward feared for her safety. She seldom locked her doors. Inside was nothing worth stealing, she averred.

As Ward pulled up into her circular driveway at the end of the lane, he had to admit that some indices pointed toward Ruth's senility. Since she was completely alone except for him, eventually he would have to consider her his responsibility, morally and financially.

Ward parked the car headed down the incline, set its brakes, and took his carpenter's kit containing his electrolysis equipment and a pint of sugar phosphate from the back seat. At the doorway, with both hands full, he shouldered his way through the unlocked front door and entered. Down the hall he could see the back door was open. Ruth was probably in the rose garden behind.

Ward set the gear in the kitchen and noticed that an electrolysis vat, with built-in cathode, anode, and step-down transformer, had been placed by the sink. Mildly

16

curious that Ruth should ask him to bring his heavier equipment when she had the vat available, Ward continued through the house and out onto the back porch.

Across the garden, by the western gate in the picket fence, he saw Ruth bent over her Scarlet Churchills, gloved, with pruning shears and a demijohn of liquid fertilizer on the ground beside the bush. He called a greeting and she waved him out to see the buds. Through a prize-winning array of varicolored roses, he walked to inspect her latest species.

For a moment they spoke of roses, hangovers, and car batteries as she completed her pruning and slowly straightened. He returned the gear to the tool box beside the western gate and she commented on the liquid fertilizer as they made their way to the house.

"The stuff seems to stimulate the quanta in photosynthesis, makes them want to jump."

Ward plucked a leaf from the underside of a bush as they passed and looked at it. "There's a substantial phytil radical, here," he agreed. "How's the arthritis?"

"Bothersome. My right index finger's so frozen I have to prune with both hands."

From long association he knew there was a tragedy behind her casual remark. She loved to play the piano. Once she had regaled the boys of Ethan Allen Military Prep with recitals of Beethoven, Brahms, and Bach to the point where an unofficial school song had been written, "Up the Bees."

Swinging stiffly up the back steps, she asked, "Ester in Frisco?"

"All night."

"Could you use some vitamin C?"

"Yes. Have you eaten?"

"No. At my age, chocolate and cookies suffice for my evening meal. My own cookies. Union scale for bakers is twelve-fifty an hour."

They entered the kitchen and Ruth gave him instructions as she prepared vodka and orange juice. "Get the bottle of absorbent from beneath the sink, put half a pint in a gallon of water with a half-teaspoonful of your sugar phosphate in the solution. But don't plug in the vat."

His tasks took longer than hers, and she had his drink poured and waiting on the kitchen table. He sat across from her.

"You mentioned one hamster, Ruth. Don't you think we need at least two? If the experimental animal dies, we'll not be sure it's a natural death."

"That's the point of my experiment. I'm having to put Papa to sleep, anyway. At our age, the hamster's and mine, timidity is a vanity."

Ward weighed her remark, wondering if she was making a philosophical observation or if she were including herself in the experiment. Surely not the latter, he decided. As a biologist, Ruth was cognizant of the delicacy of human cellular structure, unless she was senile. Then her safety would be his responsibility.

"I've allotted five minutes for amenities," she said, "so take your drink to the lab and bring me the hamster in the corner, the grizzled one that won't huddle."

Ward walked down the hall to the rear room and went over to her pen of hamsters. Five were huddled together in one corner, but the sixth, gray with age, stood alone in a separate corner, its head against the wire netting.

Ward brought it back to the kitchen where Ruth waited. "Take the rubber gloves from the cupboard and plug in the vat."

As Ward obeyed, Ruth cuddled the little animal to her cheek and said, "Good luck, Papa."

She handed it to Ward and said, "Dip him in the solution."

Ward obeyed. The little animal was too feeble to wriggle but lay docile in his hands as he submerged it. He held it under, all but its nose, for three minutes, and Ruth said, "That should be enough. There's a towel under the sink. Dry him carefully and return him to his pen. Watch him for a moment and tell me what he does."

When he took the hamster back and placed it in the pen, it waddled over to the group, sniffing among them.

"Congratulate me again," he said to Ruth when he returned. "My solution eliminates antisocial tendencies."

"That's just the beginning of the beginning, Alex. Now, I want to cure the arthritis in my right index finger."

"I don't know if it's advisable, Ruth."

"Nonsense. I use the absorbent constantly. We know the sugar phosphate's harmless, and there's only one volt of current in the vat."

She wasn't senile, so her finger was not his responsibility. He said, "Be my guest."

He stood beside her as she dipped her index finger in the solution. She held it there as he watched.

"Any pain?"

"There was, but it's going away."

She held the finger in the solution for three minutes, took it out, wiped it on a paper towel, and flexed it in front of his eyes. She could touch the heel of her palm with a finger she had not been able to bend for fear of breaking it.

"Congratulations, Alex. You've found a cure for arthritis, but you won't get the Nobel Prize without explaining the process."

She turned and faced him.

"The finger was a test run, Alex, and only the beginning. I want to take a sitz bath."

"Oh no, Ruth." His voice was jocular but adamant. "I don't mind you losing your finger but we can't risk your pelvic area. It might affect your genitourinary tract."

"I foresaw your objections," she said. "On my writing table in the living room is a signed, unconditional release relieving you of all responsibility in the experiment."

"Ruth, you couldn't clear me, morally or legally, if the side effects are fatal."

She took his arm and the eyes looking up into his were not those of the woman who had warned and commanded him for the whole of his adult life. They had lost their authoritativeness and in them was a plea, profound and pathetic.

"Alex, I've had too much pride to burden you with complaints, but arthritis isn't fun and games. Have you ever wondered why a woman with my mind stays stewed during her waking hours? Pain! One year of life as a functioning, pain-free woman is worth more than a decade of this."

Though smiling, Ward shook his head. "It might make you pregnant."

"I'm twenty years past menopause."

"Nevertheless, I can't risk you. You're half of everyone I love."

"If you really loved me, Alex, you would grant my request. Look at this hand . . ." She flexed it before him. "Once more I can play the third movement from Bach's *Passion*. After that, if my arm fell off, I would still consider myself rewarded . . . I'm a condemned prisoner awaiting a slow and painful death, and you have the keys to my prison. Set me free, Alex."

Her fervor and her logic touched him, and he smiled to hide his pity. "You give the orders."

"Spoken like a true son of Ethan Allen Prep. Get in there, boy, with your electrodes, and draw my bath, half a tub of water, one pint of absorbent, and one teaspoonful of the solution."

While Ruth went to the bedroom to undress, Ward set up the anode and cathode at opposite ends of the bathtub and drew her bath. He had no fear of electrocution—the transformer permitted only a four-volt flow of direct current—but he did fear side effects from an experiment on a human being. Ruth was his coequal in biological science, but her judgment could be warped by pain.

It occurred to him that he should stand by while she bathed, but there was a question of objectivity involved. In his youth when Ruth was beautiful, Ward had indulged in tea-and-sympathy imaginings about her that went several furlongs beyond sympathy.

Ruth solved the problem by entering in her bathrobe saying, "Out, boy. Out."

He stood for a moment outside the door waiting to hear a thump, a gasp, a cry for help. All he heard was a splash and gurgle.

"If you need me," he called, "I'm right outside."

"Nonsense, Alex. Put a pan of water on for chocolate . . . If the sun is down, you can turn on the light in the kitchen."

As a widow on a professorial pension, Ruth was sparing of electricity, and the forty-watt bulb in the kitchen added little to the twilight as Ward set water to boil. Within ten minutes, she skipped into the kitchen, toweled and robed. At first glance, it looked as if nothing had happened, until she bent before him, touched her toes with her fingertips, straightened quickly and swung from side to side, moving freely on all joints. Her face was so radiant with joy and freedom from pain that he spontaneously reached out and embraced her, holding her fragile, once-tortured frame with gentleness.

"Ruth, when you came out of there, all radiant and unshadowed by distress, I knew that if I should live to be one hundred this was my finest hour."

"Pshaw, Alex," she hugged him gently. "This was a joint effort. Your sugar phosphate would have been worthless without my absorbent. Now, let me get the chocolate started. This is just the beginning, Alex."

As a schoolboy studying geometry Ward had always tensed when reading in Euclid the phrase, "It is, therefore, self-evident . . ." Whatever followed was usually incomprehensible. Now he was becoming likewise leery of Ruth's "This is only the beginning." As she turned to the stove to prepare the chocolate, he sat down at the table feeling some trepidation.

At the stove, she spoke in trivialities to dull the poignancy of the moment.

"The way to make chocolate properly is to prepare a thick mixture, almost a wet fudge, of hot water, sugar, and chocolate and let it set awhile on a low flame before you add the warm milk. Mix the ingredients carefully, stirring all the time, back and forth, back and forth, with a swishing circular movement, smoothly, gently, never breaking the rhythm. You've got to have rhythm."

Out of respect and habit he paid attention, but Ward could not have cared less how to make hot chocolate. Besides, she seemed hung up on the phrase "back and forth," which she kept repeating as she stirred.

Finally, she adjusted the burner to very low and turned back to the table to join him. She took a sudden quick sip, looked over at him, and said, with obvious effort, "Alex, you know I'm on your side."

"My side?"

"Your side. I've never intruded on your personal life, but Ester's too much woman for you to handle, boy. She steps out on you."

Ruth was intruding, but he feigned polite surprise.

"I suppose the husband's always last to know."

"Never trust a woman under fifty. Ester's a high-stepping strutter. Did you ever wonder why she doesn't have children?"

"She goes along with me," he said. "I haven't time for children and we both are concerned about the population explosion."

"That's not your reason, either."

Suddenly he was interested. He had read about subconscious psychological motivations, but he had never tried to apply the theories to himself.

"What's my reason, Ruth?"

"Psychologically you're fixated on a breast level, and you don't want to share her breasts with a child."

Ruth was wrong. He was quite willing to share Ester at any time other than every other Tuesday.

"What's Ester's reason, if not ecological?"

"Sex! Oh, there are other reasons, engineering problems, perhaps, but basically she can't take time out from her hanky-panky."

"Engineering problems?"

"If Ester had children, her breasts would fall. Then she'd need a block and tackle to get into her brassiere, unless she was willing to push those things around in a wheelbarrow."

"I follow your reasoning, Ruth, but I'm not quite clear how the reasoning got started."

"Your happiness, Alex. I told you I'm on your side."

"I'm happy. Sex is Ester's problem."

"You can solve it for her."

"How?"

"Get in there and take a sitz bath. No sense letting it go to waste."

"I have no arthritis. You volunteered as guinea pig, and I . . ."

"I'm neither a guinea nor a pig, and you can check that with Ester when she gets back from San Francisco."

Intuition had pointed Ruth to Ester's current lover, and Ward veered from the subject. "I haven't observed you long enough to determine side effects."

"If you're waiting for me to die, Alex, I can tell you now that death is not a side effect . . . You're happy, but I want you to be happier. So get in there and take your sitz bath. It won't hurt you. All it does is correct the random error process, which I'll explain how after you've taken your bath."

He did as he was told, partly from habit and partly from curiosity about the theory of random error. He felt sheepish in the bathroom as he stripped and dipped into the tub. It was a waste of electricity, and sitting in used bath water made him feel squeamish.

After five minutes, his squeamishness passed. Ruth had honored him by permitting him to use her bath water. If he had been a true friend, he would have watched over her as she bathed. She would have understood if he had felt a residual kickback from his childhood fantasizing. Even now he could feel impulses from his memory, so he focused his attention on another slight mystery.

He had to ask her why she had called a cure for cancer "bush league."

After ten minutes, she called him. He got out, dried, and dressed. Back in the kitchen, he found the table set with a dish of his favorite home-baked macaroons placed in the center of the table, not six or seven, but at least a dozen.

"Feel any different?" She asked.

"Not particularly," he answered honestly. "But I'm anxious to hear about this random error theory."

She seated him and brought the chocolate, sitting across from him.

"Random error is an accumulation of defective DNA in non-dividing cells which impairs performance of the cell—the aging process. Your solution plus my absorbent plus an electric current adds enough missing rungs to our broken ladders to repair the damage from this process, almost instantaneously."

"How does this affect Ester?"

"Alex, you theorist! Don't you realize that bathtub in there is the Fountain of Youth? You now have the genito-urinary tract of a sixteen-year-old boy."

His first thought was that she had gone dotty, but fear for himself and loyalty to her canceled the thought. In her desperation and pain, she had become vulnerable to nostrums and was practicing faith healing on herself.

Then he thought of Ester's problem, Ruth's really, since it had never bothered Ester.

"How will this help Ester?"

"Biologically the ideal mate of a thirty-two-year-old woman is a sixteen-year-old boy. Ester's three years over the hump, and you're back in prime."

Ward munched a macaroon and thought.

"Within any group," he reminded Ruth, "there are individual variations, and I was a virgin until I was sixteen."

"Nonsense. You lacked inspiration earlier. You had outgrown your mother; and Ester, at that time, I suppose, was breastless."

All this emphasis on breasts upset him. A normal man didn't love a woman for her bosom any more than he loved her for her earlobes. Ruth seemed to have the fixation, not he.

"Ruth, I'd better head home. Ester always calls at midnight to see if I'm safe."

She glanced at her watch. "It's only a little past nine. You can help with the dishes."

"Thanks for the macaroons and chocolate. They really hit the spot."

"Hit the spot, huh?" she said, rising to take the dishes. "I can tell by your innuendos you're feeling peppier already. Grab a towel, boy, and lend a hand."

It was a delight to watch her clear the table with such ease after her halting movements before. Whether healed by faith or by the solution, she flowed and rippled with the grace which had attracted the cadets of Ethan Allen Military and Preparatory School. When he reached beneath the sink for the drying towel, the back of his hands brushed her thigh, and even his knuckles told him that she had good muscle tone. Despite her age, digging around in the garden had kept her muscles firm.

He was standing beside and slightly behind her and she was bending over the sink when she said, "Alex, I hate to think of you going home to that empty house. Don't you ever feel lonely? Don't you ever get blue?"

Sadness in her voice triggered an impulsive show of affection. From behind her, his arms circled her waist and he kissed lightly the skin of her neck.

"Not so long as I have the mother of my spirit. I hope Professor Gordon appreciated a wife so wise, compassionate, and judicious."

She held his arms against her with one hand and reached back to stroke his cheek with the other. Her hair held a faint scent of lavender.

"He never tried to get me elected to a judge's bench, if that's what you mean."

He chided himself for using abstract terms. Despite her logical mind, Ruth was a woman, and any woman preferred a compliment to her hairdo over praise of her mentality.

"When I was a boy, I thought you were the most beautiful woman I had ever seen. Despite the age difference, if it had not been for my reverence for Professor Gordon I would have stood beneath your bower banging on my banjo until you consented to a bit of old New England bundling."

Her breath seemed to catch at his alliteration of "b."

"Watch your Oedipal feelings, Alex."

Beneath his right palm, her stomach muscles were hard and resilient. He patted them, affectionately. Her faith in her rejuvenation was drawing him into the orbit of her belief.

"I have a theory why Professor Gordon died young," he said.

"I'm a pragmatist," she said. "Demonstrate."

He moved closer.

"Well, that's not an invitation to a game of pinochle," she said. "At my age it's monstrous to have such thoughts, because you're still the boy I met thirty-one years ago, my fresh-faced, smiling student; but even then you were teacher's pet. We shouldn't be standing here like this. If you're going to misbehave, Alex, I'm going to send you to bed. No, Alex. Don't kiss my lips. I forbid you. Come, young man, you're going right to bed."

With his arm around her shoulder·and her arm around his waist, the two old friends walked from the kitchen with a slow, ritual movement as if they approached some pre-destined altar before which friendship would be offered the supreme sacrifice. So rapt was Ward with the ripple of her thigh muscle against his that he forgot to turn out the light, and she forgot to remind him.

"Thirty-one years, boy, is a mighty long time."

Before them, the long hall seemed endless, and he stepped up cadence as her remark lowered the weirs of his own long-pent and ill-recognized longing. In a spate of words, his dark secrets flooded out.

"One of the boys in dormitory C, we called it master-batorium C, drew your picture on the wall, and going to the john was called 'going to see Ruth.' Dear lady, you'll never know how many lonely offerings were offered to you by the boys of Ethan Allen Military Prep. As first among your acolytes, I made Portnoy look like Little Lord Fauntleroy."

Finally, in the soft forty watts from the bedroom ceiling, she unveiled the inspiration which in the shadows seemed as lissome as a girl's. Memories touched on memories at the sight, and as Ward divested himself of impediments his verbal gusher continued to blow.

"Perhaps my subconscious reason for choosing Ester was to exorcise your litheness from my heart, for your maidenly swellings mock the pneumatic bunnies on the center-fold spreads."

In the dim light he spoke the truth, for she appeared boyish and appealing. He sat on the edge of the bed, lean-ing over her and gazing down at her ageless beauty.

"You're more than merely woman, Ruth. You're sister and spouse, sweetheart and friend, brother and sister, son and daughter."

She smiled at his extravagance, "Thanks for omitting

grandfather, but let's not weigh this moment down with confessions. Thirty-one years are preliminaries enough."

Obediently he turned to her and noticed a peculiarity which brought again to his mind the trite image of baby's bottom.

"Ruth, you surely don't pose in the nude for photographers."

"Pubic baldness, Alex. I'm seventy, but now, mine eyes have seen the glory la-di-da-di-da-di-da."

She hummed a few bars of the "Battle Hymn of the Republic," and when she swung into "Tiptoe Through the Tulips" he discovered he was not the only one with dark secrets. Doctor Ruth Gordon, champion of Beethoven, Brahms, and Bach, was a secret lover of pop rhythms.

"Drifting and dreaming, la-la-li-la . . . Soon, I'll be sailing, la-ta-ta . . . Sock it to me, daddy, ta-ti-ti-ta. John Henry's a steel-driving man, hup-hup . . ."

Her practice was so distracting that he tried to break into her titles and humming with a remark, "By golly, Ruth, you're the best seventy-year-old woman I ever knew."

"Hoped I might be the only, but you can't have everything, la-ti-da . . . Waiting on the levee . . . Come on along, come on along, Alexander . . . La cucaracha, la-li-la-la-la . . . Tralala boom de ra!!! So long, It's been good to know you . . ."

One adjusted. In fact, her announcement of the title of the next melody helped alter his tempo, and on the third movement, which proved to be the coda, he was singing along with her.

When finally he had to depart, bending above her to kiss her good night, he asked, "Ruth, why didn't you let me kiss you in the kitchen?"

"My jawbones are brittle, and I couldn't risk my bridge."

"Your sacroilliac's quite limber," he commented.

"My rhythm was a little off," she said, "because of long widowhood."

"No. You're everything we dreamed of in Dormitory C."

"Thanks, but run along, Alex. You've got a schedule to keep and I've got some heavy thinking to do. You've got the biggest moral decision that ever faced a man facing you, and I want to make the right choice. Get cracking on your theory tomorrow, and I'll work on social implications."

Inadvertently, he was humming the Brahms lullaby as he closed the bedroom door behind him and walked down the hall to the exit. Ruth had always been an influence on his life.

He remembered his gear in the bathroom, but he knew it would be no problem for Ruth to put away now she had rid herself of arthritis. He would come back for it when he had more time.

He closed the front door and went to his car, remembering his weak battery. Below him, Pinyon Verde Lane was illuminated and deserted of traffic. He cut the brake and rolled a block, coasting to get the car started, then switched on his lights and drove home, analyzing the evening.

This event had been more than an illicit liaison. Possibly her arthritis had been hysterical, and not sugar phosphate but long friendship and mutual regard had been the catalyst which prompted his extended performance. Ruth's action had been inspired by a psychic overload of affection built up from years of caressing only hamsters. Despite overtones of self-deception, the experiment had been fruitful, relieving Ruth of her imagined arthritis and demonstrating his own freedom from breast obsessions. And to his knowledge it was the first time sex had been used as a tool of pragmatism.

Ward got home in time to take his call from Ester.

He told her of the rose garden, of the flamboyance of the Scarlet Churchills, of the crunchiness of the macaroons, of the thrill of coasting downhill in the dark. It was a beautiful story, although he edited the triple denouement. Fervor touched his words, for when he closed, Ester said, "Honey, you sound like Tuesday night."

After they hung up, Ward was troubled by Ester's reminder. Next Tuesday was his night, and after such a Saturday night he would have to cancel unless he started his homework early. Ruefully he went into his study and returned to bed with a folio of paintings, drowsily leafing through the lithographs.

Suddenly his attention was drawn to a familiar nude by Rubens, "Venus Reclining." Cupid flitted above the sleeping female with his bow drawn, and the artist had captured a tension in the bowstring Ward had never noticed before. It was the direction of the arrow, really, which created the drama in the string. On the couch, Venus was only feigning sleep; he could tell from the expectant half-smile on her lips. She knew where Cupid was aiming his arrow, and the target was ready.

"By golly," Ward breathed, now fully awake, "Peter Paul Rubens was a pornographic painter."

Church bells awakened him in the morning. He rushed through breakfast to get to the lab quickly, then had to call a taxi because his car wouldn't start.

Ward chose laboratory over church on Sunday because he felt that working with protein molecules brought him closer to God than singing hymns off key. This Sunday's work, to explain God's ways to the Nobel Awards Committee, would be particularly sacred.

Outside, a Sabbath quietness lay over the campus, the air was balmy, and a jacaranda tree bloomed beside his door. He felt communion with his microscope as he slid a slide of fragmented DNA under the focusing lens and gazed on the mulligan stew of life. He stroked the positive switch, watching the fragments come together, stop, come together, stop, like shy and inexperienced lovers.

Remembering with pleasure Ruth's idiosyncrasy of last night, he tapped out "La Cucaracha" on the key, making the elements dance toward a union. In rhythm, they circled to find each other, sugar to phosphate, cytosine to guanine, thymine to adenine. When the parts of the helix were almost in place, Ward held the third beat conventional for the rhumba.

But the elements of the assembling molecule did not stop with the current.

"Tarara BOOM de ray!"

Guided only by inertia of rhythm, with the current on

"off," the elements leaped toward one another in a spontaneous, self-willed creation of DNA ladders.

Ward was stunned. He shattered the nucleic molecules with a negative flow and re-ran the experiment. He had seen aright the first time. When the sides of the ladders were in close proximity, moving to a set rhythm, they leaped to interlock.

Suddenly Ward knew what had happened on the slide, knew why, and knew there was no language by which his knowledge could be verified.

The key was environment, and the rules were universal. Thymine and adenine loved each other with the passion of valence, and they coupled in a two-hydrogen bond of marriage to form the DNA, family for the cell, nation, which formed the body, civilization. All this was tender and true, but how did one convert sex appeal into a number and solve for sentiment in an equation? What was the prime factor, the ultimate unity, and what math could explain organic affinity?

First, one created a symbolism combining the abstractions of mathematics with the metaphors of literature . . .

Ward's phone rang. Ruth had decoded the DNA, read "hamster," and was ready to give him hell. He decided to head her off at the pass as he picked up the phone.

"God speaking, Creator of Life."

"My God!" It was Ester and angry. "You parked your clunk in the drive and I couldn't get my car into the garage until I called the service man for a new battery."

"I'm sorry, dear. It was stupid of me."

"Your stupidity is no excuse. You're going to be punished. I'm modeling my new mini-nightgown before you tonight, and locking you out Tuesday."

She always berated him when she came in from a tryst as if she were projecting her guilt feelings onto him, so he had to plead a bit to placate her. Ten minutes after he quieted Ester, Ruth called.

She didn't mention hamsters, but asked, "Have you considered the social and economic implications of immortality?"

"You handle the bookkeeping. I've got my own problems."

"Your youth juice can bridge the generation gap, permit the dialogue to continue, person-to-person. But I'm not sure about publishing, even for a Nobel Prize. This is a military secret. Table your paper until I okay the release."

"Table it? I haven't yet determined the prime factor in the system of symbols."

"Then go ahead on the theory, but keep your notes locked away. Have you any more liquid in the shop?"

"Over two gallons in the store room, but it's marked 'cleaning fluid,' and I'm the janitor around here."

"Good. But don't mop the floor with it."

She hung up and Ward turned back to his blank sheet of paper.

Somewhere there had to be a key, a prime factor, expressing the basic affinity, some obscure conversion factor which would unify all force fields, gravitational, electromagnetic, electrical and organic. With a sinking feeling he remembered that Einstein died searching for a Unified Field Theory, and Einstein had not known of organic force.

At dinner, Ester glowed with reports of a darling little tailored blue suit and a matching hat with a sun visor for which she would have to return Wednesday for additional fittings. Ward could have easily listened for half an hour, but dawdling over coffee created no symbols and launched no metaphors. He excused himself and went to his study.

When Ester entered at eleven for her good night kiss and to model her new mini-nightgown, he was no closer to a symbol or metaphor than before but he was grateful that the gown was pink chiffon and not police blue.

As she swirled before him, the extreme thrust of her mammae threw the gown into billowing disarray which created ripples in the fabric that gave a liquefaction to her thighs, wholly visible on the pirouettes. She resembled a painting by Degas made animate in a style more graphic than that he had discovered in Rubens. On her final pirouette, she bowed, turned, and ran trippingly from the study with a final flirt to her bottom.

That little twist did it.

Squealing, Ward leaped after her. In vain she fled into the bedroom and sprang to the safety of her bed, but with a bound he caught her. In a swirling froth of pink chiffon, the Great God Pan was alive and rutting in the Ward bedroom, and strangely, Ester did not resent his animality. Before she walked in shreds to her dressing room, she said accusingly, "You've been taking lessons."

Seated beside the pile of pink fluff, taking off his shoes, Ward berated himself for his ungentleness. He got up and went to his dressing room to undress and prepare for bed, knowing his energy was depleted for the night. Anyway, he comforted himself, it could have been worse; something besides her nightgown could have caught in his zipper.

Slipping into his silk pajama tops with the Nehru collar, Ward heard the vacuum cleaner whine. Contrite and bottomless, he rushed to lend a hand, but the last pink thread was vanishing from the counterpane. Ester, clad in a conventional nightgown, hooked up the attachment and turned to roll the cleaner back to the broom closet.

"I'm sorry, dear," he said, coming to take the handle.

"Sorry!" she whirled on him. "I'm proud that you fell in love with me. You've got more surprises than a box of Crackerjacks."

Her arms were moving around his neck in an invitation to an encore which he unmistakably accepted even as he considered her expression "fell in love."

It was a quaint term based on Newtonian gravitation which had been modified, though not invalidated as a concept, by Einstein's world lines. Ester's nearness was both a curve and an attraction, a gravitational world line interlocked with his own. By extension, if space were curved and the universe finite, as the General Theory seemed to indicate, then infinity was a unity encompassed by a master world line enclosing circles in circles.

"By golly, Ester. Here I've been fooling around with the parts and never studied the whole."

"This is rather unusual," she said, "but, if you insist, you may go into the study."

Ester was unaware of a breakdown in communication until Ward's whiteness vanished in the darkness and his footsteps dwindled down the hall. Perplexed, she felt that her husband, rushing to his study in Priapean urgency, might be yielding to some strange compulsion, possibly academic, to make love to his desk. On tiptoe she followed him; she wanted to see how he pulled this off.

Then she heard his voice, pitched high with excitement, speaking into his recorder: "In the mathematics of affinities, the universe is assumed to be a closed system. Thus, the symbol for infinity is considered the symbol for the master affinity, the universal world line, or the total environment. Thence, it is self-evident . . ."

Quietly Ester returned to bed and turned out the light, knowing all was well with her husband.

CHAPTER THREE

.

Ward's Saturday night and Sunday, too, was not proof of rejuvenation, but the fact that he was out of bed by six, Monday morning, and at work in his laboratory before seven indicated youthful energy. Once at his desk he worked as a man possessed and by ten had established a formula to account for last night's satyriasis:

$$S^{(2)} \times P = C^{(2)}$$

With his new system of emotio-mathematics he could establish formulae rapidly because he was choosing the symbols. In the formula above, S represents an organic force field, male or female, generated by hormones in a state of dynamic balance with C, or centripedal force. Therefore P represents the proximity factor.

His animalism had been the product of the rapidly collapsing force field, $C^{(2)}$.

On the first Monday, Ester slept till noon and arose to fire the maid. She prepared dinner Monday evening, and he got in four solid hours of work in his study before yielding to Ester's P factor. Thereafter Ester couldn't sleep because of the energy generated in her force field by his collapsing world lines, and she did housework between 1 and 5 a.m. On the other hand, Ward's dissipated S induced languor and he slept.

Tuesday morning, Ruth called him at work and invited him up for a noon snack of chocolate and macaroons. She wanted his opinion on her survey of the social problems of immortality.

"Ruth, I haven't time. At the moment, I'm converting Aristotle's *Poetics* into the linear equations of esthetics."

"But I need your opinion. I'm so immersed in these problems I haven't been out of my library since early

Sunday morning. My Scarlet Churchill was supposed to bloom Monday, and I haven't seen yesterday's roses."

Ward thought he recalled a pop song called "Yesterday's Roses," and he said, "I'm no social thinker."

"Not all the problems are social. For instance, would there be a traumatic shock when one watches his generation grow old and die? And what would be your reaction to Ester, forty years from now, when she's grown old and halt and you've still got rhythm?"

Now Ward was positive her largesse would include more than chocolate and macaroons. If he came down from the hill, drowsy and incapable on Tuesday, of all days, Ester would know why and be devastated. Ester had faith in his fidelity as he had trust in her loyalty, and his first responsibility was to his wife. Ruth had entered upon a relationship knowing he was a married man, knowing that his contractual loyalty was to Ester, etc., etc. Firmly but gently Ward reaffirmed the married man's priorities.

"Ester's a variation from the norm," he said. "Age cannot wither nor usage stale her infinite variety."

In the sudden silence, Ward realized his implied comparison, deliberately invidious, had hurt a sensitive mind unschooled in the clichés of adultery.

"Alex," there was a catch in her voice, "you've never said anything like that to me."

Neither had he said it to Ester: Shakespeare had said it about Cleopatra. Hurt in her voice aroused his compassion, and in her ignorance of Shakespeare an opportunity to console her without exerting mental effort.

"You didn't want me to talk, Saturday night," he reminded her, "but Ester's going on another shopping tour tomorrow and I know a small cafe where there's candle light and vodka. If I can take you there, I'll breathe to you such lines would smite the general ear with envy, for yours is the stuff that schoolboys' dreams are made of.

"When in the columns of the *San Francisco Chronicle* I read descriptions of the jet-set belles, I know the gilded concubines of Greeks cannot outshine the loveliness you master now . . ."

For seventeen minutes, while he solved for the esthetics

factor on the paper before him, he plucked from memory appropriate lines from Shakespeare to beguile her and closed on a line of pop music whose connotations he knew she would catch. "I'll come and get you in a taxi, honey."

Obviously he had healed her hurt, for she exploded with gusto, "I'll be ready 'bout a quarter past eight."

Nevertheless, Ruth's request prompted him to think of the ecological effects of immortality, and his first equation had frightening implications. Within five generations the planet would be choked with human beings. Nothing short of nuclear holocaust could overcome even the short-term effects of practical immortality.

On Wednesday morning, he called Ruth and expressed his fear of the maternal instinct. Fortunately he caught her in a libidinal low, for she was curt.

"Tend to your theories, Alex, and don't let it bother you. I've solved that problem. In the first place, there's no maternal instinct. Motherhood is an acquired trait. And there's such a thing as biological controls. Remember Doctor Knipling and the screw-worm flies of Curaçao."

Knipling, he recalled, eradicated screw-worm flies, a cattle pest, on Curaçao by introducing sterile, irradiated males into the species. The human problem was the female as long as motherhood existed in a near-symbiotic relationship with sentimentality, forgetfulness, drunkenness, carelessness, and licentiousness.

In the matter of maternity as instinctual versus learned behavior, he would get a grass-roots opinion from Ester.

Carrick called him at two, and the department head sounded disgruntled.

"I dropped by your house at noon to say hello to Ester, but she didn't answer."

"Ester fired the maid," Ward explained. "Housework keeps her busy until four or five in the morning, so she sleeps in."

"I didn't know things were so bad, but, with your larger grant, you can put her back on the payroll along with my boys."

"Then you've decided on the larger grant?"

"It's still under advisement, but it's getting less so. Give Ester my regrets."

Ward left the laboratory an hour early to spruce up for his date with Ruth. Arriving home, he was surprised. On the dining room table were candlesticks, clean linen, and a wine bucket containing a bottle of Thunderbird '68.

From the kitchen, Ester called, "Is that you, dear?"

"Yes, darling. I thought you were going to town for a second fitting."

"I decided that dark blue was too depressing . . . Go and get ready, dear, for dinner."

He turned to go upstairs, wondering what to do about Ruth, when the phone rang. He answered it, but it was Joe Cabroni sounding more disgruntled than Carrick.

"Get me Ester."

"Sure, Joe. Hang on."

He buzzed Ester on the kitchen extension and heard her pick up the phone.

"Where in the hell have you been?" Cabroni asked. "I've been waiting at this bar since four-thirty."

"Oh, Joe. I completely forgot our appointment in the rush of preparing dinner for Alex . . ."

Ward hung up.

When he returned downstairs, Ester was ready to start serving, but she was worried. "Joe's unhappy. I promised to have a drink with him before my fitting. Now, he's up there, getting stewed on vodka, and he promised he'd keep calling here until I join him."

Wine soothed her. The soup was delicious, and she was serving the salad when the phone rang.

"You answer it, Alex. Tell him I had a nervous breakdown."

A plea in her eyes overcame his trepidation, and he arose and went to the phone. "Doctor Alexander Ward speaking."

For a moment he could hear heavy, angry breathing and then the phone clicked.

"He hung up on me."

It was an unsettling episode, but he composed himself over salad. After all, Joe Cabroni was not Normandy

Beach, and Ward had survived stronger antagonisms. To allay the tension, he asked, "Darling, if you could keep forever young, with no body changes, would you like to be a mother?"

"If I could stay as I am, forever, I would grow boys spaced five years apart to keep a fresh crop to entertain me after you've gone."

"That would be incest," Ward pointed out.

"Of course, but what is incest if it isn't mother love gone hog wild? And grandmothers can be fun, too."

The phone rang again and Ward answered promptly. "Ward, here. What the hell you want?"

Again the heavy breathing, less angry but far more irregular, and the click.

"This is sheer harassment, a police technique to keep you on edge, and he's drunk," Ward said, returning to the table. "Where were we? Oh, yes. You were having sons by your sons' sons . . . After a thousand years of inbreeding, genetically, you would be practicing self-stimulation."

"Oh, no, Alex. I'd have someone to talk to."

Guttering candles sparkled in her eyes as she envisioned eons of ecstasy. Ward realized he was not getting a grass-roots opinion, but one of her ideas was thought-provoking. Without mortality as a basis for morality, there might be a direct ratio between lewdness and longevity.

Over dessert the phone rang again, and Ester's eyes flared in outrage. She lunged at the telephone, picked it up, and said into the mouthpiece, "Listen, you. I'm having dinner with my husband whom I love and who loves me. You can quit harassing us and you can forget that date, you vodka-swilling pig. If you call this number again I'm going to swear out a peace warrant. My husband explained your technique and I know all about you . . ."

Suddenly Ester held the phone in her hand and looked at it in bewilderment. "The bastard hung up on *me*."

Ward glanced at his wrist. It was precisely 8:15.

By now, Cabroni had passed out and the call had come from Ruth. If she judged him by the implications of Ester's remarks, he had violated the first canon in the ethics of adultery, he had told all to his wife and laid the blame for his lechery on his mistress.

Early the next morning, Ward telephoned Ruth, giving the signal—ring, hang up, and ring again. She didn't answer. By ten he was engrossed in a mathematical definition of electricity, but he remembered to call again. At lunch he ate a peanut butter and jelly sandwich and called her twice. She was still sulking, so he gave up. He would wait and let her call him as she chose to throw off her peevishness.

After lunch he became thoroughly engrossed in a definition of organic electromagnetism, plotting from Riemannian geometry in kinematic time and equation which amalgamated space-time, gravitation, electromagnetism and organic chemistry. Ward was aware that he was defining the *corpus Dei*, but all was secondary to the sheer fun of theoretical mathematics.

By five he had completed substantiating the rejuvenation phenomenon, but ecological doubts still nagged. He wondered if the maternal drive was a function of E_4 (Ego enhancement) or of S_{16} (Love). The sub-sixteen defined love as a variable of sex attraction in an area somewhat more specific than hallucinations and self-delusions. S_{16} had, at least, the reality of a rainbow.

He was scribbling a few tentative equations on his pad when a voice asked, "Are you Doctor Alexander Ward?"

Glancing up, he saw a girl in the doorway outlined against the purple of the jacaranda; the resonance of her voice vibrated with the sound of bees in fields of summer. Her pullover cashmere sweater matched the bouffancy and color of her ash-blond hair, her blue skirt matched her eyes, and the starched white collar of her blouse, folded back over her sweater, her bobby sox and saddle oxfords were of a fashion he had not seen at Stanford since the late Forties.

Ward was surprised. His laboratory was an annex behind the school of biology away from the main campus. With luck he might go for days without seeing a student.

"I'm he, but what bright whim of chance has brought you here?"

"At the registrar's they told me where to find you. I do hope I'm not intruding, but you're the only biology professor on the campus. All the offices were closed. I wanted to enroll as a freshman, next fall, and I though you might suggest preparatory courses I might take this summer."

Poised in the doorway, she was ready to turn at his dismissal or enter at his invitation and to do either with dignity. Her beauty, modesty, and poise diffused an aura of a more gracious era, a time of picnics in the park, boating, and serenades from summer pavilions. She projected into him a sense . . . Of what? Of belonging?

"You need a student counselor, miss." He smiled. "This is a research laboratory."

"Oh, dear. I'm always interrupting something important. Please forgive me."

She turned to go, rippling with a reminder of green leaves shimmering over mossy dells. Some weird nostalgia in her loveliness affected him, arranged his thoughts into iambic pentameter.

"Wait, miss. Forgive me if I seemed aloof, but students always frighten me at first. I fear they'll ask me questions I can't answer. So when I saw a girl materializing from a purple haze of jacaranda, like someone stepping through a door from summer, I had to shift my thoughts from mathematics and in the lag I lost myself in silence. Please do come in and have a seat, Miss . . . Miss?"

"Aphrodite. Diana Aphrodite," she said.

She turned to his sofa beside the door, and he was happy because he wanted her to stay awhile. In her presence, his S sub-sixteen was dropping closer to the sub-four range and limning more precise boundaries to his love concept. Her P factor operated with compelling force.

"The name means huntress, does it not, of love?"

Seated, her torso balanced at the waist, her knees together, her manner suggested stays and taffeta and high-buttoned shoes.

"Don't you think we all seek love, Doctor Ward?"

"So I've heard said, by poets and by saints, but love

may be a gentler name for lust, since both lead lovers to the self-same end."

"Semantics apart," Diana asked, suddenly intent, "have you found love?"

"Well, I am working on the problem." He tapped the equations on his desk. "But I can't truly say I've found an answer. Love seems to be a curve that climbs beyond the bounds of my graph paper. Of course, it's motherhood that's chief offender in a geometry of curving space."

She interrupted him with a laugh which tinkled with cowslip bells. "If it's fertility you're speaking of, then fatherhood is equally offensive. If you could find some devastating lure to draw men to the arms of older women . . . But then you're tricking nature."

"I'm not expert in such matters," he smiled, "but I sincerely doubt that there's a Gresham's Law of Love which states that better drives out good. Still, I must compliment you. I've never met a girl so young and yet so practical."

"Oh, I'm not practical at all, Doctor Ward." She glanced through the doorway. "I've fallen hopelessly in love with your jacaranda tree. May I spread my sleeping bag beneath it, tonight?"

"I'd feel safer if you'd unroll your bag inside. You still can see the tree through the window."

"For your peace of mind, Doctor Ward, I agree."

He helped bring her gear from the car, a white Porsche with a California license plate parked in the students' area, and encouraged her talk merely to hear her voice. She was from the East, originally, and she was interested in biology, mostly as a science. Inside he showed her the refrigerator, in case she wanted a sandwich during the night.

Before he left, he promised to take her to breakfast in the morning.

Driving home, Ward contemplated his encounter. Perhaps he had seen prettier girls on the campus, and there might be ballet dancers who moved with more grace, but Diana Aphrodite overwhelmed his imagination with a sense of lost summers, of furbelows and parasols, of fecundity and ripening. Odd, he thought, but a girl

Diana's age should have reminded him of springtime, a time of sowing. And there had been the timeless sense of belonging he felt in her presence.

Somewhere along the curve of time he might have loved Diana Aphrodite. In a circular universe with a limited number of patterns to reality, powerful affinities would cluster and repeat. If his intuition was correct, he might have been her lover as late as the 1890s, probably during some church picnic in the park.

Suddenly it occurred to him that his sense of belonging might have been a sense of familiarity. If Diana's ash-blond hair had lacked the gloss and resilience of youth, if her eyes had lacked their sparkle, her voice its fiber . . .

Ward was pulling into his drive when the parallels struck him, and he backed out, returning to the lab and driving with a haste that almost exceeded the speed limit.

Diana Aphrodite was the young Ruth Gordon.

Ruth had submerged herself in the electrolytic bath and returned to her youth, and her question about his loves had been a test which he had failed. He had given a theoretical reply to her query when she sought a personal answer.

Forty minutes after his departure, he re-entered the lab office to find her gone. All that remained of her was a hand-printed note atop his working papers.

THANKS FOR *EVERYTHING*, LUKE HAVERGAL.

Stunned by his sense of loss, he still alerted to the underlined word and went to the broom closet. His two gallons of sugar phosphate were gone.

Ward sat at his desk, wondering.

What madcap scheme had prompted her to take enough solution to renew her DNA for ten thousand years? None but a maniac would grunt and sweat under such a load of life. Of course, she realized the molecules were unstable and she could end it all with reversed electrolysis, but why had she undertaken the journey in the first place?

If she had done it out of pique over his imagined rejection of her love, she was not making her punishment fit his crime. Or perhaps she intended to continue her self-styled dialogue with the young on a face-to-face basis.

"Fatherhood's equally offensive."

Her sentence popped into his mind and with a revelation.

An inveterate pragmatist, Ruth was taking this method to prove to him that biological controls could be applied to human population. Using older females as a lure, she was going to work Knipling's experiment on the screwworm flies of Curaçao in reverse.

As a theoretician he was prepared to accept her thesis. Her grace and beauty still lingered in his mind, the first ever to inspire him to speak in iambic pentameters. But, still, it would take at least one hundred thousand females, nubile but infertile, with the enthusiasm of youth plus the skills of experience, seeded throughout the country to flatten the population curve. She had only enough solution for five hundred.

Besides, a control group of five hundred rejuvenated females would demand an equal number of competitive young women and perhaps three times that many young men to establish the superiority of infertile nubiles in open competition beyond statistical doubt. Normal human beings would never participate in such an experiment, which would demand resources of money, subjects, and space beyond the reach of an impoverished Ruth Gordon.

His mental skitterings slowed. She couldn't set up such an experiment, and she knew however feasible and personally desirable, practical human immortality was more dangerous than a nuclear holocaust.

Fingering the note he held before him, he wondered why she had called him Luke Havergal.

Of course! She wanted him to follow her. Luke Havergal was the character in Robinson's poem who had been summoned to his grave by the ghost of the girl he had betrayed. In the symbolic language of the poem, the dead girl had beckoned her lover "to the western gate."

A vision of the young Ruth Gordon floated into his mind's eye. Her grace, her loveliness, her many-faceted mind opened vistas of high romance to his imagination, possibilities of a human love no legend could approach. But such thoughts, he realized, originated in his genitourinary tract.

He owed Ester something, and with his wife so eager

to handle his in-fighting for him, he could not leave his cloister and go back to a youth he had barely escaped from alive. Ruth knew this.

Besides, she had taken all of his solution, and it would take him three weeks to process another batch. She had not told him what absorbent she had used, and she had not told him where she had gone.   ·

Oppressed by a sense of loss aggravated by guilt feelings, he tossed the note into the wastebasket. He had loved her and lost her, but he would not go back and there was nothing she could do to make him go.

Friday morning, Detective Lieutenant Joseph Cabroni arrived at his office and checked his mail. There were the usual follow-ups from incoming all-points bulletins for fugitives who might be heading for San Francisco. And he read the first paragraph of a letter from a Mexican girl pleading the innocence of her jailed boyfriend. He tossed the letter into the wastebasket. She had spelled his name "Cabrone."

A plain postcard typewritten from Palo Alto held his attention.

Lieutenant Cabroni, it may interest you to know that Doctor Ruth Diane Gordon, professor emeritus of gerontology, Stanford University, failed to attend the Sunday meeting of the Three-B club and the Tuesday meeting of the San Jose Rose Growers Association.

Obviously written by an educated person, it was no crank note, and the implication was clear; Ruth Gordon was missing. He remembered her as the old woman under the grape arbor with Ward looking at pornographic pictures during the cocktail party before he got the brush-off from Ester. If Ruth Gordon would stay missing a little longer, Ward might be held as a material witness and Cabroni would have a clear shot at Ester. Since she had gotten so damned loyal and faithful, she might be willing to contribute a little something to her husband's release.

Cabroni's ordinary procedure would have been to call

the Palo Alto police and have them check out the report. Instead, he called a newspaper editor he knew and asked the editor to check all information in the morgue on Doctor Ruth Gordon and Doctor Alexander Ward.

In a few minutes, the newsman called back. "Joe, we got a volume on Ruth Gordon, an egghead with business brains. She bought into nursing homes right after Medicare and made a killing on her specialty, old age. Besides seventeen homes for the aged up and down the coast, she's got a beauty ranch near Malibu, a topless bar in Inglewood, three boarding houses in Haight-Ashbury, two drive-in theaters . . ."

"Send her file over," Cabroni interrupted. "What about Ward?"

"Nothing, but there's a reference to his doctoral thesis in an article on the random error theory of aging Ruth Gordon wrote for our science editor."

"What's his thesis?"

"*The Conductive Effect of Electromagnetic Attraction in the Hydrocarbon Bonding of Unstable Protein Molecules with an Emphasis on Ribonucleic and Dioxylnucleic Helical Configurations.*"

"Where can I find a copy, and what subject would it be filed under?"

Cabroni found Ward's thesis in the science library at San Francisco State and spent all of Saturday and most of Sunday, with a science dictionary by his side, reading it. By midnight Sunday, Cabroni was as well versed as any officer in the SFPD on DNA, RNA, and the random error theory of aging.

Saturday evening in his study, Ward ran through his day's mail and came across a picture postcard advertising a discotheque on the Sunset Strip in Los Angeles, the Electric Daisy Chain. On the back, typewritten, was a line:

Ask Big John for the Roman Venus.

Some prankish colleague whose education in mythology was lacking had sent it, he first thought, because there was no Roman Venus. He had turned his attention back to a set of calculations beginning with $SA^{(2)} \times P + St = 0$, where St represented the sterility factor and the zero was a cipher of chilling implications, when it occurred to him that the Roman equivalent of the Grecian Venus was Aphrodite.

He tossed the postcard into his wastebasket.

Monday afternoon, on his way to Palto Alto, Cabroni picked up a no-knock warrant from a justice of the peace in Belmont and went directly to the house on Pinyon Verde Lane. Observing the letter of the law, he lunged at the front door with his shoulder and almost fell into the hallway. The door was unlocked.

Inside, on Ruth's desk he found her release of Ward for any responsibility in her death, which he photographed. In the desk he found no documents indicating her financial holdings but he found a peculiar album of family snapshots. In the bathroom he took shots of the bathtub with the electrodes still in place. All hamster pens in the laboratory were empty. Outside in the rose garden, drawn to the spot by a spade leaning against the fence, he found a plot of freshly dug loam three feet wide by six feet long.

Cabroni scooped a shovel of the dirt and his spade hit adobe hardpan six inches below the surface. For a moment he leaned on the shovel. Of all the frame-ups he had spotted in his fifteen years on the force, this was the most amateurish. Yet, there was enough circumstantial evidence here to send Ward to the gas chamber if an investigator didn't probe too deeply. Whether Cabroni fitted the frame around Ward or not would depend on Ester.

At the moment, the investigator was more perplexed by Ruth Gordon's motives.

Cabroni went seeking an eyewitness the only place one might logically be found, at the house across the cul-de-sac from the Gordon residence. A woman, thin, pale, with bulging eyes given an Oriental slant by her tightly pulled bun of hair, opened the door to his knock. Cabroni introduced himself and told the woman, a Mrs. Moresby, that he was investigating the absence of her neighbor, Doctor Ruth Gordon. Mrs. Moresby's eyes seemed focused on a distance fourteen feet in front of her, but she invited him into the living room.

Beneath a vase of rose stems, sear and leafless, her television set was on. She turned the volume down, slightly, saying, "Yes, strange things have been happening over at that house. But if you don't mind, officer, I'd like to keep an eye on *Life Can Be Beautiful*. I don't want to miss this episode."

"Go right ahead, ma'am," he said, taking a seat on the divan to her right as she seated herself before the set.

"I can look at you, too, as I talk. My bun gives me good side vision. Those roses on the TV are from Ruth; she brought them over last week, but she forgot to put water in the vase."

"Did you notice if she had any callers Saturday?"

"Yes, sir. A tall blond man in his late forties, must have been, because he had a haircut. He parked in front of Ruth's house, headed downhill for a quick getaway, and took some tools into her place. I could see right through the house with the sun behind it and not miss a thing on TV. It's my side vision. The bun does it. Well, he put his gear in her kitchen and went out back and got Ruth. They came in together and I couldn't see anything . . ."

"What time did he arrive, ma'am?"

"Seven-thirty-two. Two minutes into Jackie Gleason's show . . . I didn't see anything interesting till Lawrence Welk, when the man went across the hall to her bathroom with his tool box and pretty soon she came out of her bedroom in a bathrobe and she went into the bathroom with him. Well, they were in there together, but not long enough to do anything. Finally, he came out, but he stood by the door of her bathroom, like he was listening."

"For how long, ma'am?"

"One Geritol commercial . . . Then, he went into the kitchen, and pretty soon, Ruth comes out in her robe, almost skipping, and she's supposed to have arthritis. Hah! Officer, if you're investigating a sex crime, I think Ruth Gordon was willing. Most of these so-called sex crimes wouldn't bear investigation, if you want my opinion."

"Go on, ma'am. Then what happened?"

"Before Engelbert Humperdink, that's ten o'clock, they came out of the kitchen. Ruth left her light on in the kitchen. Something she don't usually do. They came down the hall arm in arm, him walking tippy-toed, like the front end of a little pig tripping to the trough, her strutting beside him as proud as a hen with a prize rooster. Officer, I was born on a farm in the Middle West and I know animals. I knew which room they were going to before they got there, and her complaining about arthritis. Hmmph!"

"They went into the bedroom."

"Yes, sir. Went and stayed, plumb through Humperdink, the eleven o'clock news, and well into Johnny Carson. A little before midnight, he comes out, not strutting, now, but walking fast. Not carrying a thing. He shut the door behind him and got into his car, but he didn't start that car. No, sir. He let it roll, sneaky-like, with the lights off, down Pinyon Verde Lane. About two blocks down, I heard him start the motor."

"Can you describe his car to me?"

"One of those little foreign cars you can't tell whether they're coming or going."

"Did you report this to the police, Mrs. Moresby?"

"Me? I'm no nosey busybody, snooping around, prying into my neighbor's affairs."

Cabroni's second interview was with Doctor Carrick.

Carrick's office was in the administration building on the campus, a corner room on the fourth floor. Though the carpet was linoleum and Carrick's desk was made of something resembling deal, Cabroni's intuition told him that the office was the academic equivalent of an executive suite.

After Cabroni explained the purpose of his call, Carrick remarked, "I haven't seen Ruth since the party, which is unusual. She generally drops by the faculty club for lunch two or three times a week."

"I'm trying to get a line on who her close friends were," Cabroni said.

"Doctor Ward's her closest friend," Carrick said, "and has been . . ."

"Platonic or romantic?"

"Doctor Gordon is seventy years old, Lieutenant. I hardly think . . ."

Cabroni cut across his protestations. "Did they ever engage in joint experiments together?"

"Unequivocally, no," Carrick said. "Ward would not let his grandmother into his . . ."

"What's Ward researching?"

"Finding that out would be a good project for you, Lieutenant. Ward never publishes. He talks only to Ruth, and Ruth talks only to her hamsters. I asked Ester point-blank what he was doing; all I got from her was . . . a dismissal."

To Cabroni, Carrick's sudden hesitancy meant a cover-up of some sort. The detective's voice flicked across the desk like a switchblade. "What precisely did she say, Doctor Carrick?"

"Well, that he was running a carpenter's shop, fixing broken ladders."

"DNA ladders?"

"Not a chance," Carrick answered emphatically, but the expression in his eyes was drifting away from the emphasis. "Any man who could do that would have an undivided share of Nobel loot in his pocket."

Slipping automatically into habitual thought patterns, Cabroni realized that here was motive for murder, if Ward wasn't willing to share the dough with a co-worker.

Cabroni's angle of attack shifted. Suddenly he became a respectful, almost humble, petitioner. "Your opinion, please, Doctor Carrick: would the repair of DNA affect arthritis?"

"Depending, of course, on the stage of the disease, the rehabilitation of gristle and surrounding muscle might have a generally beneficial . . ."

"Would it act as a sexual stimulant?"

As Carrick considered the question, Cabroni studied Carrick's face for subtle signs of his thought processes, a narrowing of eyes, a quivering of the underlip.

Carrick's face sharpened. His eyes grew speculative, then calculating, then predatory. His rotundity of body, formerly suggestive of joviality, changed; his shoulders became squarer, his stomach flattened and expanded upward into his chest cavities. Leaning forward, talking to himself more than to Cabroni, he looked powerful, formidable.

"If the cellular structure of the genitourinary tract were reconstituted, in toto, there would be rejuvenation, complete and pristine. The organs would be young and yearning again, possessed of a vitality that would dominate the hypothalamus, crush all psychic blocks to the libido. The discoverer of the process, had he any business acumen, could make millions, for he would possess the greatest aphrodisiac in the world. No, billions . . ."

"Thank you, Doctor Carrick, and good day."

"Princes and potentates would lay their treasures at his feet. Frustrated wives of impotent husbands would lay pounds, Reichsmarks, yen, rupees, zloty, kronor and flowers . . . The greatest aphrodisiac in the world. Generals, premiers, presidents, nations, commonwealths, empires . . ."

Quietly Cabroni closed the door and hurried from the outer office. The day was wearing on, and he wanted to get to Ester and question her before her husband got home. Because the clues pointed so clumsily to Alexander Ward as the perpetrator, Cabroni did not believe Ruth Gordon had been murdered, but, professionally, Cabroni was willing to assume Ward had murdered her. Too little suspicion could be fatal; too much never hurt.

CHAPTER FOUR

Twenty minutes later, Cabroni composed his face in hostile lines and rang the Wards' doorbell. Ward should be easy to intimidate. Most professors, even the new New Left professors who advocated violence, disliked violence when it was directed at them.

"Joe, you beast!"

Ester had opened the door and squealing with unfeigned delight she flung herself around his neck. Unprepared for her friendliness and spontaneity, his arms went around her, but she slipped from his embrace, took his hand, and led him through the house toward the bar, chatting, "I could forgive you for calling when you're drunk and obnoxious, but I found it hard to forgive you for hanging up. Nobody does that to me."

"Ester, I was drunk and maybe obnoxious, but I didn't hang up. Twice on your husband, yes, but never on you."

"Then someone else got an earful," she commented, gliding behind the bar. "I'm sorry, all I can give you is a screwdriver because Alex will be home soon."

"Is that your handiwork?" He waved toward the table in the dining room with its linen, candelabra, and gold-plated china.

"All mine. I fired the maid. Alex thinks I've grown domestic, but it's really that I don't want another woman in the house." She lowered her voice and leaned toward him. "Joe, he's so rampacious lately, a wholly new Alex with an extra added ingredient."

"Something the mad scientist discovered in his lab?" Cabroni asked.

"Maybe, but I think I had a lot to do with it. When he starts taking that little half-step, coming toward me like an adagio dancer getting ready to jump, I shiver . . .

Imagine, my own husband . . . Joe, do you love your wife?"

"Not too often," Cabroni admitted. "Having three children took the prance out of her."

"Ration her, Joe. Once every other Tuesday might do it. Strew a few photographs around of Greek statues, without fig leaves, and don't lose patience. It took me five years with Alex, then, suddenly last Sunday, wham!"

She came around the bar and perched on the stool beside him. She wore a peasant blouse and her eyes glowed with intellectual fire which suggested to Cabroni that Ester might yield to a commonsense approach.

"Ester, a girl with your resources should spread it around. How would California and Arizona feel if all the water in Lake Meade was cornered by Las Vegas? You're too much woman for one . . ."

A peculiar squeal sounded from the front porch, and Ester shot from the stool, clearing the split-level into the living room with a gazelle's leap. Cabroni turned back to his drink on the bar, thinking a little sadly how love fled.

Arm in arm, husband and wife advanced across the living room and Cabroni, turning, could see that Ward was prancing tonight. He envied the couple their domestic bliss. No doubt about it, there was something captivating about Ward's walk. He envied Ward for it, envied him for Ester, and as they tippy-toed down into the dining room, Cabroni's envy died in self-revulsion as he caught himself almost envying Ester.

Ward was more open, attentive, alert than he had been when Cabroni saw him last. The hand he extended in greeting matched Cabroni's in its grip. Murder sometimes did this to a man, Cabroni knew, by releasing his aggressions and frustrations.

"I'm glad to see you and Ester patch up your little mis-understanding, Joe."

"I'm not here to patch up misunderstandings," Cabroni said formally. "Doctor Ruth Gordon has been missing since Saturday night."

"You were supposed to be up there, Saturday night, pruning roses." Ester said.

"I talked to her last Wednesday," Ward blurted.

"Were there any witnesses?" Cabroni asked.

"Not to a telephone conversation," Ward answered, catching himself.

"Doctor Ward, she was last seen alive on Saturday night." Cabroni stressed the "alive."

"I know," Ward said. "I left my gear in her bathtub."

"What were you doing in her bathtub?" Ester asked.

"That's what I'm here to interrogate him about," Cabroni said.

"I was treating her for arthritis," Ward said to Ester.

"She's believed to be murdered," Cabroni said.

"By whom?"

"For the record, there are no suspects, yet."

"I mean, who believes she was murdered?"

"I do," Ester almost screamed. "I believe you did it to her in the bathtub and she drowned."

Moaning, Ester staggered back and fell into an over-stuffed chair.

"The official theory holds she was electrocuted," Cabroni said.

"Control yourself, Ester." Ward turned to his stricken wife. "Joe's from homicide and he takes murder seriously . . . Joe, that's my gear in her bathtub, almost three hundred dollars' worth. And if you haven't found Ruth's body, she isn't dead."

"A corpse is no longer needed to establish the corpus delicti," Cabroni said.

"I told you you'd been practicing," Ester sobbed. "I had faith in you, Alexander Ward."

"Ester, please," Ward squatted before her, "you've got every reason to trust me that I've got to trust you. Why should I practice on a seventy-year-old woman when the campus is full of co-eds?"

"Because it's furtive, that's why. Sex is no fun unless it's furtive."

He leaned forward and kissed her, and Cabroni noticed an immediate change in the tempo of her sobs as Ward turned and looked up at the detective.

"Joe, I'm worried about Ruth, but I can explain the electrodes. Let's go up there."

Cabroni considered the request. Ward was putting on

an act that might convince a rookie. If he continued the act, volunteering to go up as a friend of the deceased, he might give self-incriminating evidence that could later be used against him without the warnings of his rights or the presence of counsel or any of that Supreme Court crap.

"Let's go," Cabroni said.

"Dinner will be ready at eight," Ester said dully.

As the two men walked toward the detective's car, Cabroni considered the turn of events. For the best results, interrogation procedures required two men, one hostile and one friendly, but caught without a partner he would have to play both roles at once. "So you were giving her a treatment for arthritis, Alex," he said gently. "That was decent of you."

"Actually she gave herself the treatment. I set up the electrodes."

This one was clever, Cabroni thought as he held the door open for Ward. Already he was twisting his story to fit the evidence.

"Were there side effects?" Cabroni asked, starting the motor.

"Yes," Ward said, and lapsed into a silence Cabroni read as suspicious, then added, "but on the whole the treatment was beneficial."

"When we find her body," Cabroni said, "we'll check the skeleton for calcification."

"If you don't mind a layman's suggestion," Ward said, "I know where I could look for her body."

"Where?" Cabroni was suddenly alert, but no expression showed in his voice.

"I would go down to the Embarcadero and look for a long line of longshoremen. At the front of the line, you'll probably find Ruth Gordon's body, and very active. Those side effects were quite potent."

Cabroni smiled knowingly. "The greatest aphrodisiac in the world, eh, Alex?"

"Her words exactly," Ward said, half astonished. A man who couldn't pronounce "hermaphrodite" had rolled out "aphrodisiac" with practiced ease.

"By the way, Joe. If you don't accept my opinion, don't

go digging around in Ruth's garden looking for her body."

Suddenly Cabroni's voice was harsh, edged. "Why not, Doctor Ward?"

"Practically every bush in that garden bears a prize-winning rose, and she'll be very angry if you dig among them. She's spent all spring pruning those bushes."

"Corpses cut no roses," Cabroni said.

"Nor do they make good fertilizer when they're arthritic," Ward added. "There's too much calcium."

For a moment, Cabroni wished he were back at head-quarters questioning some ghetto kid who could answer only yes or no. After he had alerted himself for a self-incriminating remark from Ward, he had gotten a short lecture on horticulture.

When they pulled up in front of the house, Cabroni said, ominously, "There's a couple of items in her office I'd like to interrogate you about, first, Doctor Ward."

Ward did not like the official sound to the word "interrogate," but he said nothing as they entered the office and Cabroni handed him Ruth's typewritten release.

To Whom it May Concern: It is my intention to con-duct an experiment using myself as the control on this day in the presence of Doctor Alexander Ward, my friend and colleague. In the event that this experi-ment results in maiming or fatality, I wish to exon-erate Doctor Ward of any and all responsibility for the results.

Doctor Ruth Diane Gordon

"I told Ruth this release had no legal value," Ward said.

"It has," Cabroni said flatly. "It might make the differ-ence between first-degree murder and manslaughter, if an investigating officer went to the D.A. in behalf of a cooperating suspect."

Cabroni walked over to the bookcase and fumbled for the family album, taking more time than necessary to let his offer sink in. "Police are like everybody else," he mused, "do them a favor and they'll do you a favor."

He returned with the family album and laid it on the

desk. He flipped the pages over. All photographs had been torn from the first section of the album. Only paste marks remained.

"There's not a photograph in the album," Cabroni said, "taken of Ruth Gordon when she was under thirty." Suddenly his voice went flat. "Why?"

Ward said nothing as he slowly leafed through the pages. Cabroni studied his profile, waiting for the lips to part, the eyes to narrow.

Ward understood why the photographs were missing. Ruth had taken them to preclude recognition of herself when young, and by setting up this "mysterious disappearance" which pointed to his complicity, she was trying to force him to follow her. Hardened criminals broke under hours of police grilling, and she knew that he possessed a secret no police department, no authority, and no official of the Defense Department should ever share.

Why had she done it? Surely not from feminine spite after Ester's misdirected remarks. Perhaps, by forcing him to follow her she hoped to cure him of his imagined breast obsession, but if she had done it for his therapy she was being damned unethical.

Cabroni saw a flicker of anger in Ward's eyes and snapped, "Out with it, Doctor Ward. What's your explanation?"

Ward deliberated a moment and finally said, "You're the specialist in solving mysteries, Joe. You explain it."

Ward continued to thumb through the album.

"Then, I'll explain it, Alex." Cabroni's voice was again gentle. "Down at headquarters, we get educated in perversions. There's a type of sex maniac who murders a female and takes along her panties or her hosiery. Later, just by sniffing, he gets a helluva charge out of what he's done. But the highbrow maniacs, the ones with imagination, take photographs to get their kicks. Necrophilia, we call it."

"You need more competent educators down at headquarters, Joe. The obsession you describe is called fetishism. Necrophilia is an abnormal love of the dead. The most interesting case of necrophilia I've encountered occurred in Florida, about forty years ago. A man spent eight years sleeping beside his dead wife at night. She was superbly embalmed, of course, because Florida's hot and humid . . . Say, here I am! She kept the original print from the Ethan Allen yearbook, *The Minuteman.* This cadet's uniform's an authentic reproduction of that worn by the Continental Army . . . Have I put on the pounds!"

"Let's go to the bathroom," Càbroni snapped.

Over the bathtub, Cabroni explained the *modus operandi* of the murderer.

"It was simple for him to lean over the old lady as she sat in the tub and flip on the maximum current switch and shoot the juice to her. As the gentle, cultivated type, he wouldn't use even the minimal violence necessary to push her head under the water."

"If he did that, Joe, her next of kin would have an excellent suit against the Electrical Underwriters' Association. That's a step-down transformer which converts alternating current to direct current, and the maximum voltage is five volts."

Cabroni recovered fast. "He used a jumpwire to bypass the transformer."

If he had done that, Ward decided, with Ruth sitting there watching him, she would have seen what he was doing and protested so vehemently the murderer would have had to use more than minimal violence to force her head under.

"Why would he have done that?" Ward mused aloud, still thinking of the jumpwire.

"To get an undivided share of the Nobel loot," Cabroni said.

Cabroni had been talking to Carrick, Ward decided.

"Money's not the object in a Nobel award," Ward said.

Cabroni had Carrick's opinion to the contrary, and he could read the genuine concern on Ward's face.

"Another aspect of this case which supports my theory that the murderer was an alleged gentleman is in the laboratory. Let's go."

In the laboratory, Cabroni pointed out the pens and the fresh droppings.

"She kept hamsters in those pens," Ward agreed, "and she let them out to keep them from starving."

"Or her murderer was too tender-hearted to let them stay and suffer," Cabroni said. "Let's go. You don't want to keep Ester waiting, all alone, at night."

Together the two men walked into the gathering twilight to the car.

"I've got a line on her murderer," Cabroni said. "Someone who enjoyed her confidence, a bathtub buddy. Probably a fellow scientist. They were onto something together, and he didn't want her to share credit for the discovery. So he eliminated her. Personally, I'm betting he's a professor at Stanford."

"That would be a very good theory, Joe, if she were dead."

"She's dead. As an old friend and fellow professor, Alex, you just refuse to face the fact of her going this way."

Only one professor on the campus fitted Cabroni's description—Ward himself. Ruth had planned it this way, but her plans had gone astray; Cabroni would get him before he could get to her. Diana Aphrodite had taken his available supply of rejuvenating solution. Besides, he did not know what absorbent she had mixed with the liquid.

They drove to the first boulevard stop on Pinyon Verde when Cabroni turned to face Ward. "What were you doing in Doctor Ruth Gordon's bedroom between 10 p.m. and midnight, Saturday, May 29th, and why did you leave her house without turning on your car lights or starting the motor?"

Caught off balance by the question, Ward stammered, "Well, my battery was weak and the car wouldn't start."

"What about the bedroom?"

"I was checking Ruth for side effects."

"What kind of side effects were you checking?"

"Well, for one thing, the arthritis treatment unfroze her pelvis."

"Alex, you aren't telling me you laid the old broad?"

There was no point in lying to protect the reputation of a woman who was branding him a murderer, Ward decided.

" 'To lay' is hardly the verb form one would use, Joe. It was more of a horizontal dance, but she kept breaking my rhythm by humming pop music and changing the tunes."

"It's honest of you to admit this, Alex," he said.

"Since I know you're a family man, Joe, who gives fittings on the side, I figure my secret's safe with you."

This one was wily, Cabroni decided. He was attempting to head off an investigating officer's testimony by appealing to male loyalty. Or was it blackmail?

As Cabroni drove on in silence, pieces began to assemble in Ward's mind: the card from Los Angeles, the Javert who drove beside him, and there had been more to the Luke Havergal reference than an invitation.

Because he had no choice, he would go to the western gate of the rose garden, take the solution she had hidden there, and follow the ghost of his first love into the jungles of the young, specifically to the Electric Daisy Chain in Los Angeles, where Big John would tell him where to find Diana Aphrodite, née Ruth Gordon.

He loved his wife, but Ester could make out quite well without him and this was a matter of prior loyalties, not to Ruth but to the continuing processes of evolution. In her youth mania, Ruth intended more than a limited rejuvenation. To widen the scope of her experiment, she needed his help and unlimited amounts of the youth solution.

When Cabroni pulled up before the house, Ward invited him in for dinner, but Cabroni declined. "No, Alex, I've got to get back downtown. I want to wrap up this case by Friday. By the way, Doctor Ward, don't leave this jurisdiction without checking with the D.A.'s office. He might want to question you . . . Enjoy your dinner."

When he entered the dining room, Ester came out of the kitchen wearing her long-suffering smile. "Your stride is off, Alex. I know what's troubling you, but I forgive you. You had your little fling with Ruth, but she's dead or gone."

"It isn't Ruth, Ester. I've been immersed in theory so long I think I should come up for air, get in some field work. Down Mexico way, they're doing some interesting work in the effects of mescaline on white mice. I think

I'll head down for a while, during the summer session, and look into it. Care to come along?"

"When will you leave?"

"Tomorrow. All I have to do is check out enough money, buy some rough clothes, a jeep, and anti-venom serum for rattlesnake bites. You'd enjoy wandering around in the desert this summer. Those landscapes are romantic with the rock and the cacti, and we could both use a little sun."

"No thanks, Alex. I'll stay and tend house."

"In that event, I have some papers I'd like for you to type and take over to Doctor Waverly-Pritchard, after you get them notarized."

Tuesday, after lunch in San Jose, along a freeway he had once feared to venture over in his VW, an organically twenty-years-old Alexander Ward tooled a green BMW 280 south toward Highway 101. A motorcycle's speed of escape made it worth the risk, he had decided, and the BMW 280 was proving his judgment. Under a blue crash helmet with wind visor, wearing a black leather jacket over a pink suede shirt with a white silk scarf, shod in hobnailed motorcycle boots, Ward felt like a bird gliding currents of concrete air, soaring over hills and swooping into valleys, banking around automobiles which seemed stalled at sixty miles per hour.

Rejuvenation and escape had been simple. Cabroni had posted no guard around Ruth's house and he had used her tub, afterward taking his equipment and the remaining solution, which were stowed in his bag on the carrier rack behind. His only difficult moment had been personal. After he tidied up his lab, and locked the door for perhaps the last time, he had turned to face the jacaranda tree in bloom. Then the poignancy of departure knifed him and he remembered a line from Hopkins.

> Margaret, are you grieving
> Over goldengrove unleaving?

Now, all sadness had been pummeled from him by the wind-whip of his passage, and youth let him lose himself in sensualities. He felt the heat of the westering sun on the jeans hugging his thighs, the bounce of seat springs, the plasticity of handlebar grips and, riding easy in the saddle, the charged bouyancy of the lance he bore to the jousting grounds of the Sunset Strip.

At intervals the heavy licorice female odor of alfalfa floated across the highway to mellow the astringency of diesel fumes. From the tank beneath him wafted the scent of gasoline, heady with nuances of speed and freedom. South of Salinas he smelled the wetness of irrigated loam and the tang of eucalyptus as the valley stroked by, and then he climbed into the oak humus smells of Paso Robles.

Atascadero, San Luis Obispo, and, toward the southeast, the Sierra Madres formed their names in his mind with the tinkle of mission bells. Winding down from the Santa Lucias, past white dunes by the sea, he came at last to the most unforgettable, unforgotten place name of all, Pismo Beach. After Pismo Beach, Santa Maria, Los Alamos, Gaviota, and Santa Barbara sounded pedestrian.

At Ventura, he swung east on the Ventura Freeway into Los Angeles after picking up a signalert on his mounted transistor radio that 101 was paralyzed from Malibu to Santa Monica with beach traffic. The Ventura was clear almost to Sherman Oaks, where it clogged for the San Diego Freeway intersection. He wove through the lanes and gunned his motorcycle east toward the Hollywood Freeway. Another signalert warned that eastbound traffic on the Hollywood was backed up two miles west of Cahuenga Pass by an accident.

From what he had heard of Los Angeles traffic, Ward assumed that "catastrophic" was an Angeleno code word meaning at least five dead. He knew that he could navigate through the jam on his cycle, but the rims and spokes of his wheels were clean and bright and he didn't want them blood-splattered, so he turned off at Laurel Canyon and went over the Hollywood Hills as the twilight turned the smog over San Fernando Valley a deep purple.

At the Mulholland intersection at the crest, Ward detoured over to Mount Olympus to get his first unobstructed view of Los Angeles.

He became concerned for classical mythology when he

saw a Grotto of Jupiter near the top of Mount Olympus, but his alarm was superseded by admiration for the eclecticism of Hollywood. At the top, he dismounted and walked to a balustrade to look over the city.

South of the Hollywood Hills, the smog had rolled out to sea and lights were coming on. The flarings of Hollywood were looped by the red-green-purples of the Sunset Strip to the glow of Beverly Hills. From the curving lights at the foot of the hills radiated the straight beacons of La Brea, Fairfax, La Cienega, and Doheney slashed by the diagonal gleam of San Vicente. Due south, the strait of lights washed against the distance-dimmed radiance of the Baldwin Hills. To his left, Western and Vermont drew dwindling perspectives into an ocean of incandescence which bent beyond the curve of the planet.

As an esthete, Ward was awed by the lights below. As a biologist he feared for the humanity served by the lights as its fate juxtaposed in his mind against that of the screw-worm flies of Curaçao. But in the vigor of his youth, he yearned toward the promise of the lights and for the girl with summer in her voice who pervaded his being, still, like the memory of an old-fashioned garden.

Fragmented, Ward remounted his motorcycle, and the warm feel of the saddle re-integrated him. One with his machine, he turned down the winding road toward Sunset Boulevard.

At Schwab's drugstore he was directed a few blocks east on Sunset to a motel where he was charged extra for a room with a view of the swimming pool.

Decorated in orange and blue, Ward's room appeared inviting at first glance, but a nameplate screwed atop the color television set warned him that the tube was protected by the Electronic Detective Agency. Close inspection revealed that a lithograph of a Russell was bolted to the wall, the bed was countersunk beneath the carpet, and a rubber aspidistra plant set in a Styrofoam pot painted to resemble terra cotta was unobtrusively chained to the wall. Fortunately, the soap wasn't screwed to the soapholder, so Ward took a shower.

A mile west from his motel on Sunset Boulevard, Ward

found the Electric Daisy Chain at a bend in the boulevard. Two and a half stories with a penthouse, the building was on the uphill side of Sunset near the middle of the County Strip between the City of Los Angeles and the City of Beverly Hills.

Sunset Boulevard along the Strip had the Western flavor of a Las Vegas without high neon signs. Business establishments fronted the Boulevard with residences immediately behind on streets that climbed sharply to the north or dropped away to the south. The commercial buildings formed a melange of shops, apartments, nightclubs, commercial high rises, hotels, hamburger joints, and expensive restaurants. Architecturally the Strip's underlying unity was chaos.

Turning behind the Electric Daisy Chain, he parked in a lot without an attendant and walked east down an alley, south down a side street, and west two doors to the discotheque. Long-haired young people, a few barefooted, milled along the sidewalk or sat on the curb. They moved aside at his approach, forming a corridor that led to the door of the club, and he heard a girl murmur, "Dig that pink suede shirt."

A placard beside the door announced the opening night of Glamorgan, the Welsh bard, for his first appearance in the United States. On the door itself was lettered:

ADMISSION FREE
NO COVER—TWO DRINKS MINIMUM

Despite the sign, no one seemed to be entering but Ward, who shoved open the door into a dimly lit foyer. To his right was a cashier's cage. On his left was a cloakroom with a girl seated behind a half-door. Ahead of him, up a short flight of steps, a uniformed security guard stood before a second closed door. On the door beside the guard was an illuminated sign: NO BARE FEET.

"You pay here, sir," a girl in the cashier's booth called.

"Your sign says admission free."

"There's a two-drink minimum, sir, and you buy your drink coupons in advance. Drinks are two-fifty apiece. That will be five dollars, sir."

Either this was a clip joint or it was in a high rent

district, Ward thought, as he drew out his wallet. He couldn't see Diana Aphrodite patronizing such a place when Ruth Gordon was so careful with money.

Ward took his tickets and started up the stairs with his helmet under his arm when the guard called down, "Sorry, sir. You'll have to check your crash helmet. It's considered a weapon."

Ward turned to the checkroom and handed the girl inside his helmet.

"That will be a dollar fifty, sir."

Ward paid because the guard, holding the door open for him above, was beginning to look imposed upon. Ward hurried up the steps and the guard asked, "May I see your I.D. card, sir?"

Ward took out his wallet, for the third time in ninety seconds, and handed the guard his driver's license. The guard flashed a flashlight onto it and flashed the light into Ward's face.

"You can't pull this trick in the Electric Daisy Chain, Haircut. Miss Frost can't abide minors who swipe their old man's license to swill booze. Give me your tickets and take these."

The guard took two chips from a pile on the ledge behind him and handed them to Ward. Ward took the chips because they were balanced on the end of his driver's license, and once he had accepted the chips he felt he had to honor the serve, since the guard was opening the door for him.

"What are the chips for, sir?"

"They entitle you to two Shirley Temples."

"But I paid for alcoholic drinks."

"Miss Frost isn't about to lose her license selling booze to minors. Move along, Haircut. You're blocking traffic."

Entering, Ward understood why there was no traffic to block. Four steps across the vestibule at the Electric Daisy Chain had cost six-fifty—over a dollar a step.

Down a hushed corridor, carpeted and lit by electric tapers on paneled walls, Ward walked, through unguarded swinging doors, into a blast of sounds without rhythm where lights swirled without illumination. To his left, through the weirdly lit shadows, he could see forms that moved fantastically to the discordant melody. He had not returned to the swinging years.

As eyes and ears adjusted to bedlam, he saw the noise came from a jukebox amplified by speakers around the huge room. To his right, dimly seen, small tables were crowded together, and beyond, in a corner, he saw a service bar. Above the floor where dancers weaved and jerked hung a spotlighted bird cage where a girl in a bikini, eyes closed, writhed to the rhythms of a very different drummer. On the floor, couples moved without touching, front to front, side to side, back to back, keeping at a distance possibly to avoid injuries, since their jerks seemed unpremeditated. After Benny Goodman, the Dorseys, and Danny Kaye, this dancing was not in his sack.

Fingering his chips, he edged around the dancers, looking for an ash-blond head in lights that made all hair red, green, or lavender, waiting for the music to end as one record followed another endlessly. Apparently, the sets were over only when the dancers dropped.

"Sit down, Establishment, and buy us a drink."

The voice sounded softly beneath the juke's hammering vibes. Turning, he saw a girl at a table almost beneath him, her hair long and lanky. She wore a T-shirt and no brassiere—a tactical error, since her chest resembled a washboard with a single corrugation.

But seated next to her was a blue-eyed blonde, exuding serenity, whose hair was fluffy and her skin well scrubbed. She wore a loosely fitted cashmere sweater which yet was strained to contain her proportions, and for her the absence of a bra was a strategic triumph. Above her magnificent left was a campaign button reading "Love it or leave it."

Ward threw his chips on their table.

Before his bottom touched the chair, a waitress was beside them, saying, "A round here, sir?"

"Two Shirley Temples and a Scotch and water," he ordered and said to the girls, "You're both too young for alcohol."

"Only Establishment creeps get their kicks from alcohol," the dirty girl said.

"You just called me 'Establishment.' Does that make me a creep?"

"Cool it," the girl said. "I meant you were anti-Establishment Establishment. What's your name?"

"Al, from Atascadero," Ward said, playing it cool. If they figured he was from the state institution there, they wouldn't ask questions. Once Cabroni found out he was gone, the name Alexander Ward might be a handicap. Since he had been employed on government grants, his fingerprints were on file with the FBI.

"I'm Margie. This is Dolores. She's fresh and clean from a motorcycle rumble."

"I'm interested in motorcycles, too, Dolores." Ward turned to the well-washed beauty. "I drove down on a BMW 280."

"Wow," said Dolores. "BMW 280."

"You shouldn't have told her that," Margie said. "She's a motorcycle groupie, and she could get you killed. What are you pushing, Al? A new hair style?"

"It's the style at Atascadero," he said.

"It's just like Papa's," Dolores said. "Nixon would love it."

The waitress brought their drinks. "That will be three-fifty for the Scotch and soda, sir, not including the tip."

"The girl in the foyer told me they were two-fifty," Ward said.

"They are two-fifty in the foyer, sir. But there's entertainment in the main ballroom. Glamorgan, the Welsh Bard, is making his debut in America in fifteen minutes. Another first by Miss Frost."

Ward tipped her a quarter and she picked it up, muttering, "All this and a suede shirt."

"Is this a clip joint?" Ward asked the girls when the waitress was out of earshot.

"Miss Frost caters to the elite," Margie explained. "All the kids here have connections."

"Well, here's expensive mud in your eye," Ward said, raising his glass.

Dolores did not raise her glass. As if she had forgotten something, she asked, "Are you a radical?"

So lately immersed in mathematics, Ward assumed

Dolores was using a *double entendre* in that rarest of all humor, mathematical wit. He quipped back. "I'm a square without a square root."

"Wow," said Dolores, wide-eyed at his repartee, and she lifted her glass in a toast.

This girl was brilliant, Ward decided. Not one female in a thousand would have caught his nuance and toasted it. And there was about her a quality—aloofness, detachment, imperiousness—which might have belonged to Joan of Arc.

"Her papa's head of the Orange County Patriots," Margie explained, "and doesn't want Dolores associating with the New Left because he's a wheel in the New Right."

"Light up, Margie, and give us a drag," Dolores said, switching the talk away from politics. Obviously she had breeding as well as brilliance.

Ward felt he had much in common with the poised, well-groomed Dolores. She was witty, averse to gabby women, and shared his interest in motorcycles. Like hers, his political bias was conservative, and they had similar family backgrounds; Ward's father had also been a strict constructionist.

From her bag, Margie produced a long, slender cigarette, lighted it, and rolled a cloud of smoke at Dolores, who ignored the gesture. To prevent a cat fight, Ward interjected pleasantly. "Is it Turkish?"

"No. Lebanese," Margie said, wafting a cloud toward him.

Vaguely Ward recalled hearing some talk about Hollywood blow jobs and he decided that Margie must be some local form of kook, a blower. To humor her, he smiled. "Very pleasant."

"Tenting tonight!" Dolores cried, and leaned over, cupping her palm under Ward's jaw and drawing his cheek to hers, tilting his head forward until all three foreheads were touching over the table. Their heads formed a triangle which caught the smoke rolling up from Margie's mouth. For Ward, the touth of Dolores's forehead offset the acrid odor of the smoke.

Ward assumed it was some sort of spontaneous group

encounter, currently the rage in California, and the sense of sharing grew pleasant in the confines of the tent. Neither Diana nor the Surgeon General of the U.S. might have approved of such behavior, but Ward hated to see the ritual end. It brought him the feeling he was in a free fall while stationary.

After their last drag Margie leaned back and said, "That stick cost me seven bucks, wholesale. You both should contribute at least two dollars apiece."

Now Ward knew he had reached the penultimate territory of the hustler, but Dolores was reaching for her bag, and so he said, "I'll pay the two dollars for Dolores."

Having worn a groove through the air to his pocketbook, Ward quickly handed over five dollars. Margie pointed to the dollar and quarter change from his drink on the table and said, "There's your change, Al."

Again he was wondering why Diana had chosen such a place, since Ruth was so thrifty, when it occurred to him that Diana might have trouble recognizing him with the music casting such weird shadows against one's eardrums and the lights blaring against one's eyeballs.

With sudden insight Ward realized what planning had gone into these small tables, because his across-the-table continuing dialogue with Margie ran concurrently with his under-the-table continuing dialogue with Dolores, who was saying, "Wow."

"I'm looking for a man named Big John," he said casually.

"Freddie the Hustler can introduce you," Margie said, turning to the mass of dancers to send a keening through the vibes.

"Fred-eeee the Hust-lerrrr!"

The name almost panicked one Ward, the depression-reared Establishment graybeard from Palo Alto and New England for whom money represented a cherished value. Anyone called "the hustler" in this milieu must be king of con men.

But the other Ward, communicating with Dolores under the table, inwardly shrugged off the name. Within him, the generation gap was narrowing, and in great measure from the example of generosity Dolores showed when she took his hand and cupped it against her. But then she suddenly removed his hand and placed it firmly back in his lap.

"Now," said Dolores, "that's for your two dollars."

The times, they were a-changing, he thought. In his day, two dollars went a lot farther.

CHAPTER FIVE

.

Out of the flickering lights came a Negro young man,
pelvis jerking fore and aft to the rhythm of the juke,
fingers aloft and snapping. If his Afro had been any
bushier, he would have needed more head.

"Freddie, this is Al from Atascadero. He wants to meet
Big John."

Freddie's eyes flicked toward Ward with an expression
verging on insolence, flicked down at the dollar and
quarter on the table, grew calculating, and looked again
at Ward.

"How bad do you want to see Big John?"

"About a dollar's worth."

"African pride won't let us Watusis work for peanuts
any more."

"Stick a bone in your nose and I'll go two dollars."

Freddie's arrogance turned to wheedling. "Make it a
dollar and a quarter, man. I'll take you to Big John personally."

"Are you selling your pride for a quarter?"

Trapped by Ward's logic, Freddie grinned.

"I'll take the green and we'll make the scene," he said,
palming the bill. "Follow me."

As they shouldered their way through the crowd, Ward
asked, "Does Margie get a percentage of your take?"

"Naw. I don't like the company she keeps."

"What about Dolores?"

"That's the company I'm talking about. Dolores looks
clean and she's not too lean, but she runs around with
boys who are mean, like hog jockeys."

"What's a hog jockey?"

"Motorcycle rider."

It occurred to Ward that he had much to learn about status symbols of the young, but Freddie's rhymes intrigued him.

"I noticed you use rhyming jive. I thought that went out of style in the Thirties."

"I'm warming up for Big John. If you want to post a message, throw him a rhyme. He'll give you top billing every time."

Suddenly Freddie was leading him into the men's room, past two swinging doors separated by six-foot intervals. Past the second door, they entered a sanctum of urinals, stalls, and white silence. Floors, walls, ceilings, and the doors of the stalls were all white-tiled, and the place was spotless.

"A woman runs this joint," Freddie said. "Her name's Miss Frost and she's queer for white and clean. But I don't take it personal. Excuse me."

As they stood side by side, Ward asked casually, "Freddie, how would you like to make five easy bucks?"

"That depends, man."

"When we get back to the table, get rid of Margie for me."

"Forget Dolores," Freddie said. "She's the Big Papa's girl and he's head of the Orange County Patriots."

Ward had read scholarly analyses of the so-called "Orange County Syndrome," and he had heard his share of liberal jibes in that area, but regardless of what the liberals said, he still considered patriotism a virtue.

"I thought you were a hustler." Ward was deliberately sarcastic.

"They call me that because I work two jobs, one here in the morning and one down the street after eleven, but I'm not setting you up with Dolores. She's high on speed and headed for a crash."

Speed was the lure Ward intended to use to get her behind him on his motorcycle, and he feared no accident on the short drive to the motel.

"All you have to do is take Margie onto the dance floor for about five minutes."

"Give me the five, but stay alive. Don't split with Dolores while we're away from the table."

It was not his intention to split with Dolores, rather the opposite. He handed over five dollars, and Freddie said, "Let's meet Big John."

Standing beside a blackboard at the far end of the rectangular room was an old Negro man, tall, slender, gray, but as erect as a guardsman, wearing a smock. Freddie swayed up to him, saying, "Big John, this is Al Atascadero. Got a Mexican name but he's a gringo."

With a dipping swing, Freddie swirled away, snapping his fingers. The old man watched him leave, saying, "Freddie's learning but it'll take time. He's got to get the beat as well as a rhyme."

Big John turned to Ward. His left eye was covered by a milky cataract, but his right flicked up and down appraisingly. For a second Ward regretted his white silk bandana, pink suede shirt, genuine leather jacket, and kangaroo boots, because he was marked as a pigeon and he had a strong feeling he was going to be hustled again.

When Big John spoke, his voice quavered slightly with age.

"I don't push horse and I don't sell gage, for I can't risk narks in my old age; but if you've got a yen to write on the wall, then step right up and buy a ticket to the ball."

He pulled a piece of chalk from his right pocket and motioned toward the board. An interesting gimmick, Ward thought, like legalized prostitution, but Ward felt no compulsion to write on toilet walls.

"I'm looking for a young woman, Big John. Her name's Diana Aphrodite and she told me to ask for you."

"She didn't mean it in a personal way," Big John explained. "You write on the board what you got to say. Then word gets around, all over town."

Now the tile had a new significance to Ward. Big John used the owner's desire for cleanliness to establish a monopoly. He had the chalk. He stood watch on the board, and from the left pocket of his smock jutted a chalk eraser.

"I assumed the management was keeping the walls free of grafitti," Ward said.

Big John snorted. "On this john Miss Frost never lays her eyes. The board's my private privy enterprise."

He pointed to the board, which had a painted line dividing it horizontally a fourth of the way from the top.

"For ten words or less left one whole day, a dollar is all you have to pay; unless you want a message easier to view, then above this line will cost you two."

Ward remembered Freddie's advice, that Big John gave rhymsters top billing.

"Big John, I'd like to give your system a whirl, but I'm trying to get a message to a girl. As a business man, you'll have to face it, the boy's room wall is no place to place it."

Big John shook his head. "All the little foxes have deposit boxes. Word gets past the wall in no time at all."

Ward was reasonably sure no long-haired hedonist would make a deposit in Diana's box, but young girls whispered secrets to each other. Besides, Diana would be waiting for his message.

"I'll pay the two for a message with a view."

The old man handed him the chalk with an admonition as he pocketed Ward's two dollars. "Write it plain and keep it clean because I erase anything obscene."

Glancing over the board, Ward mused aloud, "Since humor's the nitty-gritty of grafitti, it's easier remembered when it's witty, but this girl is fond of myth so I'll make ancient lore the pith."

"Man, you'll pass," Big John blurted in admiration. "That's classic gas."

Above the line, someone had out-hustled the hustler with a compound word to cut down the count: "Filmore, I'm becoming dreadfully afraid of Virginia Werewolf. Please, rescuemefromherpad."

Above the plea for help, Ward lettered boldly, "APHRODITE, DIONYSUS IS HERE AND IS LONGING FOR YOU."

When Ward returned to the table, Freddie seemed to be in an argument with Margie, for he was saying vehemently, "Dolores, I'm no bagman and I don't handle dolls. It's like I'm tired of hearing 'Up against the wall.'"

"What wall?" Ward asked.

"Man," Freddie said, "I could be rock-hunting in the Mojave and out would come a helicopter, full of pigs and dangling a wall. Next thing I'd hear would be 'Up against the wall, you black mother-lover!'"   ·

Freddie finished the phrase, shouting into silence because the jukebox had suddenly gone dead.

"Glamorgan cometh," Margie said.

Ward groaned aloud at this delay. He had forgotten the premiere of the Welsh Bard in the United States in his concentration on Dolores.

Margie heard him. As the lights dimmed, she said, "I dig all Glamorgan's platters. His voice is like touching in a nude sensitivity-encounter group. It's way out."

In total darkness, Dolores leaned over and whispered to Ward, "Dionysus, wow."

Ward was amazed and disconcerted. At this rate of progress, his message should be in Venice West in another five minutes, and Diana might find him before he escaped with Dolores.

But the room was pitch dark, now, and silent with expectancy. Ward found himself tensing forward in the dark, waiting.

Suddenly a lute sounded three clear notes. A pencil-thin spotlight scratched the black and diffused slowly around Glamorgan, seated on a stool on the go-go platform, from which the cage had been lifted. Profile to the audience, hunched forward over his three-stringed lute, he gazed down in awe and wonder at his own instrument.

"Get a load of those eyebrows," Margie whispered.

Somewhere a girl screamed as Glamorgan turned to his audience, a gentle half-smile on his lips. His hair fell to broad shoulders and curled under a page boy hairdo which framed a wide and rugged face tapering to a delicate, pointed chin. A pink shirt opened to show his marble neck.

Gazing down on his audience, Glamorgan's eyes glowed

with a sweetness—Ward couldn't think of a better word—
and his sensitivity mixed with his massiveness to project
the impression of a masculine angel.

Glamorgan spoke.

In lilting Welsh accents, the Bard explained that he had
come to "Amerikah" to sing of simple yet enduring things,
the touch of hands, butterflies fluttering, of mayflowers
blooming on Brecon, and of a love once found and lost
on the road between Merthyr Tydfil and Ebbw Vale.

Glamorgan sang.

His voice was an alto sounding tones of purity and
simplicity which swung his audience into rapport with
his sentiments, and, strangely, Ward felt himself drawn
by the singer's tenderness and delight in simple things.
However, Ward parted company with Glamorgan after
they reached Ebbw Vale.

Glamorgan sang a ballad, about a lass picking berries
in the bracken, which he announced as his own composition, but Ward recognized the melody from an old English folk song, "Strawberry Fair." Ward's sense of fairness
so turned him against the otherwise pleasant lyrics that
he failed to applaud the performance.

At the finale, Glamorgan sang to his lute another "original" composition:

> My lute, awake! Perform this last
> Stanza which we have now begun,
> For when this song is sung and past,
> My lute, be still, for I have done.

In a ritualistic bow, Glamorgan bent before his audience, and, in the silence before applause, indignation
wrenched a shout from Ward's throat.

"Your galley is loaded with forgetfulness, Glamorgan.
That envoy was written by Thomas Wyatt, 1503–1542."

The dimming spotlight was focused on the bowed head
of Glamorgan, who raised his luminous eyes toward his
heckler's voice. His lips twisted and his alto screeched in
accents which Ward, who had spent a sabbatical at Cambridge, recognized as Liverpudlian.

"Up your bloody arse, perfesser!"

Then all was dark. Ragged applause arose and died with the rising lights, and Glamorgan had vanished.

"You ruined his act, Al," Freddie said. "Miss Frost is up yonder, watching. If it hadn't been dark, she'd have you whiteballed from one end of the Strip to the other."

"Not unless management countenances literary and artistic theft,"   .

"Wow," said Dolores.

Freddie nodded to Ward, and said, "Hey, Margie, I learned a new Afro dance. Like to do it?"

"Groovy."

As the jukebox blared again and the lights started to spin, Freddie led Margie onto the dance floor.

Ward stretched lazily and turned to Dolores.

"I had a bad trip down from Atascadero and I've got to spin rubber back to my pad. Could I see you home on my BMW 280?"

"BMW 280, wow!" Dolores was dreamy with excitement. "But my papa wouldn't like it."

"You have to declare your independence sooner or later."

"But he's coming to get me."

"Maybe I could talk to him. I'm not a bad sort."

"Maybe you could, Al. You talk different."

"Let's try it, anyway," Ward rose and took her arm.

Through flickering darkness where strobes danced to the vibes from the juke, he led her into the quietness of the corridor. As his eyes adjusted to the steady light from the wall tapers, Ward looked at his prize. She seemed to float, her feet barely touching the carpet, as if helium filled her breasts.

He said, "Dolores, you have a lovely face, and you walk with buoyant grace."

"He's been to the john," she said, explaining his inadvertent rhyme to herself. "They always talk like that when they've been to the john . . . But he said you had a pretty face . . . Nobody ever says nice things about my face . . . He's not a teat man, Dolores."

A mild touch of schizophrenia, Ward decided. A spin in the night air would be just the thing to bring her all together again. He could understand her feeling. He had felt a schism within himself after their communal smoke.

At the checkroom, he picked up his helmet and enjoyed the comments on his pink suede shirt when he tipped the girl a dime.

Outside, the moil of sidewalk people again formed a lane for them, but now the youngsters looked on Ward with sadness. From somewhere, he picked up a feeling of final things and held Dolores closer to him, thinking perhaps his mood sprang from a subconscious fear of hepatitis.

As they turned up the side street, Dolores asked, "What day is it, Al?"

"Tuesday."

"I mean like is it yesterday or tomorrow?"

"Today's today."

She looked at him with a concern approaching fear. "That's what I was afraid of. I got to meet Papa. I was hoping it was yesterday. I didn't see Papa yesterday, because I'm fresh and sweet."

Ordinarily Ward might have wondered about her confusion, but his hand supporting her arm was far enough down that his knuckles touched her breast, and Ward felt like some prehistoric saurian with two nerve centers. The message from his knuckles warped the impulses from his brain.

In her innocence, Dolores had lied to herself in the corridor. He was a teat man. Ruth Gordon had been right about his obsession, but Dolores was in worse shape.

"Your attitude's abnormal, Dolores. Your father shouldn't be so protective, and you shouldn't let him be. An Electra complex can lead to complications. Your father should see a psychiatrist."

"My father is a psychiatrist."

"Then he lacks insight . . . Freddie told me your papa was in politics."

"He is."

Well, Ward thought, the two professions did overlap in certain areas, and perhaps her father needed more help than she. Buoyed by the thought of making love to this splendid girl in a three-way manner, therapy for him, for her, and for her father, Ward was prancing when they rounded the corner of the building and headed down through the parking lot.

Suddenly Ward spotted a Schweinjaeger 605, first in a line of motorcycles angled backwards against the wall. He whirled Dolores around to inspect the machine, all of its details visible in the overhead light of the parking lot. It had double chrome mufflers with a bank of triple headlights, the center one a spot, and a tandem seat with a leather-upholstered backrest and safety belt. Instead of the conventional chain drive, it had a stainless steel differential rod.

"Look at this," he breathed in admiration to Dolores, noticing below them three motorcyclists lounging against the wall, each with his right boot sole propped against the bricks in identical fashion, each with helmet slung on the right side of the belt.

The Schweinjaeger's speedometer was set for r.p.m.s rather than miles per hour, the mark of a quality product, but Ward thought the owner had overdone the decorations. Raccoon tails dangled from the handlebars. A decal of an American flag was pasted on the side of the gas tank, and, circling, he could read on the mud guard: SUPPORT YOUR LOCAL HARD HATS.

One of the loungers left the wall and approached Ward and Dolores, walking with a crab-like sidling, keeping his left thigh forward. Probably a victim of a traffic accident, Ward thought, as he drew nearer. He wore a crew cut, Ward noticed before the man put on his helmet. Most of his hair was in his heavy, scarred black eyebrows and tufting from his nose and ears.

Deference seemed appropriate, as the man was almost thirty, over six feet tall, and nearly half as wide across the shoulders.

"Is this your bike, sir?" Ward asked, smiling.

The man's helmet also displayed an American flag, and sewn above his right pocket was a blue strip holding three white Navy stars with red centers. He didn't return Ward's smile, and his voice rumbled, "That's my hawg."

"Whatever you call it, it's beautiful."

"Take a good long look, boy. Most likely it's the last you'll ever see . . . You all right, Little Mama?"

"I'm coming down too fast, Big Papa," Dolores said. "I'm going to get the agonies."

"I'll get you to a brewery, directly . . . Honey, has this Pinko been molesting you?"

"He's not a Red. He's Al. He wants to ask you if he can take me home."

"All the way to Orange County? Little Mama, you know you can't tell it when you meet a Red. They're subversive." He swung his massive head toward Ward. "Whose home you aiming to take Little Mama to, Pinko?"

With sickening certainty Ward realized he had misread the situation. Both Freddie and Margie had warned him, but he has assumed the Orange County Patriots were merely conservatives. Dolores was the mama of a motorcycle gang.

All Ward could rely on, now, was his charm, reasonableness, and the community of interests created by a mutual regard for motorcycles.

"Hers, Big Papa." Ward smiled. "She seemed confused, disoriented . . ."

"Careful what you say about Little Mama, boy."

"But I felt she needed protection, and . . ."

"Then you must have figured she had something to protect. You been thinking dirty about Little Mama, boy?"

Ward's situation demanded a desperate remedy.

"Big Papa, you don't understand, but . . ."

"You saying I'm dumb, boy?"

"I'm saying I was trying to get to you, because . . ."

"You calling me a queer, boy?"

"Listen, Big Papa. I'm a short-hair, like you. I drive a motorcycle, like you. I voted for Goldwater, and I want to join your club."

"Well, boy, why didn't you say so?" A grin gave the face a coarse magnetism and Ward the hope that he might be getting through to the man.

"Arms, Lefty," Big Papa's voice rumbled among the parked cars. "Fresh meat!"

He turned back to Ward.

"If you want to join the Patriots, you got to prove your loyalty. Let me see your helmet."

Ward handed his helmet to Big Papa, who stood sideways before him. Big Papa pivoted around to his side bag and pulled out a decal.

"Little Mama, lend me your head."

Little Mama walked up to Big Papa and he put the helmet onto her head, adjusting the chinstrap. Carefully positioning the decal, he adhered it to the front of Ward's helmet and stood back to admire his handiwork, saying, "Real nice, honey."

Two young men emerged from among the cars. One wore a short-sleeved leather jacket because his biceps were too large to fit a normal sleeve and the other, one-armed, carried a car radio in his hand. They had flags on their helmets but wore no stars.

"Boys, meet Al. He wants to join the Patriots." He turned to Ward. "You understand, boy, before you take the loyalty oath there's a security check, initiation fees, and a haircut."

Lefty had laid down his radio and he sidled around in front of Ward, saying, "I'm Lefty, Al," and extending his left hand as Arms extended his right, saying, "I'm Arms."

Ward extended both hands and the two did not let go after they shook hands. Instead, they pinned his arms to his side. Ward resented a trick that had made him a prisoner by presuming on his friendliness and goodwill, but fear dominated his resentment. Not since the Normandy landings had he felt such dryness of mouth and urgency of bladder, and a phrase from his youth kept recurring to his mind, "Keep a firm sphincter, Ward."

"Ball Bearing, front and center," Big Papa called back toward the wall loungers, and one broke away from the wall, sidling up with the crab-like motion which Ward now assumed to be some cabalistic ritual among the Patriots. He wore two stars above his right pocket.

"Ball Bearing here!" He reported in a voice almost cultivated.

Ball Bearing was a slightly built man with large gray eyes and sandy hair and the thin line of a mustache. With an air of remote detachment about him, he reminded Ward of photographs of the young William Faulkner.

Big Papa looked Ward up and down with a slow, implacable contempt as he spoke to Ball Bearing. "Two-Star, this Red conspirator is the clumsiest would-be infiltrator into the Patriots I ever saw. He tells me he voted for Goldwater and he thinks I'm dumb enough to buy a cover story that would make him about eight when he voted. But I'm not charging him with disrespect. Take him down in the corner. I want him tried and found guilty of intent to lay. When he rounded that corner he was pussyfooting in front of Little Mama worse than she did the day I got the Schweinjaeger . . . Now, I got to get Little Mama to some candy before she crashes."

Other black-jacketed men wearing kidney belts were sidling out from among the cars, they, the men, regarding Ward with that same hostility and circumspection their leader had shown, not saying anything but merely looking with expressions at once both contemptuous and profound, as if they saw Ward at the epicenter of some soundless fury around which they had swirled from the day of their birth and around which they would be moving in mindless rage and frustration until they lay dying.

There was an interlude of silence as Big Papa strapped Dolores into the tandem seat, still wearing Ward's crash helmet, and roared off down the alley. Quite deliberately, the two had conspired to steal his helmet.

Two-Star turned to Arms and Lefty. "Take him down into the corner . . . Brazos, front and center."

The last man against the wall came over and said, "Brazos here." He wore one star. He had the Texas look—the leathery, wind-beaten face and high cheekbones of a cowboy and Indian.

"Put Hoot Owl on the west and the Loon on the east end of the parking lot . . ."

Two-Star was giving instructions as Ward was led down into the dark corner of the alley. As they passed the line of motorcycles, the Patriots started the motors and set them on idle. Thoroughly concerned, now, Ward hoped the rumble of motors might merely announce that court was in session, but he was self-possessed enough to realize that there might be other reasons for the noise. One might assume, for instance, that this was a kangaroo court and the roar was designed to cover the thud of fists against flesh. From the major premise it would then follow that the fists would be theirs and the flesh his.

When Two-Star returned to the group, accompanied by Brazos, his voice sounded soft and reassuring beneath the low rumble of the motorcycle engines when he spoke to Ward.

"Son, there's nothing personal about this trial. We Patriots believe in law and order. Our Three-Star, Big Papa, has given us the order to try you for intent and his order is law . . . Breeches, give him a security check."

Again Ward's wallet left his pocket.

"Patriots, is this Commie loaded!" Breeches said. "Credit cards from here to yonder."

"Count his initiation fee, Breeches," Two-Star said, "and you, Razor, check Breeches while he counts."

Turning to Ward, Two-Star said apologetically, "These pre-trial proceedings take a little time."

"Eight hundred and twenty dollars," Breeches whooped. "This Commie's a capitalist."

"Liberate it," Two-Star said.

Ward recognized the terminology from World War II. He was being robbed. Anger built up in him at his helplessness and the men who were taking advantage of it, but despite his anger and his fear, his mind absorbed and weighed every detail, his memory recorded each name. Still, he could not understand the sideways stance the men adopted when facing each other.

The answer came from an unexpected shout of warning.

"Guard your crotch, Al!"

The cry keened over the tops of the parked cars, and

looking upward toward its source he saw Freddie the Hustler atop a delivery van.

"Get that black bastard," Two-Star said.

Four of the Patriots separated from the jury and swung out through the cars, but they wore hobnailed boots and Freddie wore sneakers. His first leap over the four-man net closing in on him cleared two autos and placed him atop a station wagon. Freddie had covered fifteen feet in a standing broad jump.

It seemed incredible to Ward that members of the same club could do to each other what these men obviously feared, but more frightening was the knowledge that he had stood vulnerable before them for so long. Figuring Two-Star, in front of him, for a right-footed kicker, Ward swung his left thigh forward.

"We're doing no crotch job on you, son," Two-Star explained with absurd gentleness. "We're only giving you a haircut."

He turned to his leathery-faced subaltern. "Where's the Barber?"

"Chasing the jig."

"Forget him, Brazos. We've got a trial to conduct."

"Barber, front and center," the One-Star, Brazos, yelled. "With clippers."

A clean-cut, helmeted youth with blond eyebrows emerged from between the cars, holding a short length of sprocket chain in each hand. He cast a casual but professional glance at Ward's hair as he, too, stood sideways in front of Ward. Ridiculous though the precaution was, Ward realized that the youth was guarding his crotch from Ward.

"How do you want him styled, Ball Bearing?"

Two-Star rubbed his chin reflectively. "All he's guilty of is the intent to lay Little Mama. That's worth only a Sing Sing or at most a modified Monk, but Big Papa was unhappy about the way he pussyfooted around Little Mama and it might make Big Papa unhappy if we let him off with less than a Mohawk."

Ward felt indignation and relief. Such young men in the past, he had read, used German storm troopers as models, but apparently the current fad was to imitate the French maquis who sheared the hair from French-women who fraternized with German occupation troops.

"A Mohawk takes a little time," the Barber said thoughtfully, "since I'd have to trim for his warlock. And we're out of our territory."

"Very well," Two-Star said. "Give him a Yul Brynner."

The Barber took his hip-forward stance in front of Ward.

"Would you tilt your head slightly to the right, Al? I don't want to clip your ear."

Since the Barber had no clippers, Ward assumed he was studying hair contours and tilted his head. He was determined to remain detached about the invasion of his person, consider it no more than an extreme prank.

Psychological shock almost dulled Ward's pain when the chain in the Barber's left hand whipped up and lashed the side of his head slightly above his right ear. To obtain a cutting motion, the Barber blunted the force of the blow with a forward jerk as the chain lashed into the side of Ward's head, but the force remained strong enough to bounce Ward's head to the left where it was lashed and swung back by the chain in the Barber's right hand striking in the same relative position. Left and right, swish-thud, Ward's head bounced with the rhythm of a punching bag.

Here was sadism, gratuitous and calculated, performed by an all-American boy in the trappings of a patriot. Ward was being scalped by lacerations at the hands of an expert. Overlap of chain cuts from opposite sides of his head was infinitesimal, and the slits were climbing toward the peak of his head in precisely parallel furrows.

With two quick strokes across the crown, the haircut was finished, and the Barber stepped back.

"You can check it, Ball Bearing, but I don't think I missed any spots."

"Tilt his head back, Patriots," Two-Star's voice was now grotesquely gentle, "to keep his blood from blinding him. Cut off his bandana to wipe his forehead . . . Too bad about that pink suede shirt. Must be an eighty-dollar item."

Over the top of the cars the voice of the dark angel called, "Guard your crotch, Al."

Two-Star's delicate concern for his shirt enraged Ward. Faking grogginess, he tottered to a sidewise position, his head lolling backward on his neck. He had been trapped by the logic of his position; in a community of violence, a man of peace must accept the life style or remain forever vulnerable to his neighbors. Ward accepted the situation and adapted to it.

Intent on his inspection, relaxed and perhaps contemptuous of his victim, Ball Bearing stood with his hands on his hips, legs spread. He was not guarding his crotch.

"His hair's matting fast," the Two-Star said, "but I see a couple of spots above his right sideburn . . . hmmph!"

With the fluidity of a striking cobra, impelled by the frustrations of a quarter-century of nonviolence, Ward kicked. His thigh propelled his steel-capped toe in a perfect trajectory and with superhuman strength. All pain was obliterated by the exultation he felt when his toe, carrying all before it, imploded into Ball Bearing's groin.

Figuring the Patriot's weight at 160 pounds and a conservative lift of four inches on the vertical and a twelve-inch movement along the horizontal plus a six-foot slide on his back after his heels struck the ground, Ward calculated that his kick would have scored a 102-yard field goal in the Coliseum.

One-Star assumed command.

"Drain Oil, you and Crank Case take No-Star over to his hog and try to revive him. He just lost his two stars, but he learned to guard his crotch."

"That's locking the stable after the stallion's gelded," the Barber said.

"He wore his helmet in the wrong place," the ape called Arms commented.

"This changes the charges to assault on a fellow Patriot," Brazos said, turning to Ward.

"I'm no longer interested in the kangaroo court procedures of you crabs on the pubes of a subculture of hopheads."

"What did he say?" Brazos asked the Barber.

"I don't know, but it didn't sound like a compliment."

Clearing the court took hardly more than three minutes. As Two-Star was carried past Ward he was moaning, "Kill me, shoot me. I'm ruined."

"Fellow Patriots," Brazos addressed the group, "you've got a new field commander, and I'm no pussyfooting bleeding heart when it comes to Pinkos. Let this be a lesson to all of you; never trust a Red, and guard your crotch. But he ain't getting off light. There's a new judgment in this here court. Boys, I'm ordering a crotch job on this subversive . . . Crotch Job, break out your long chain. Breeches, you handle the breeches. Sprocket, left ankle. Razor, right ankle. Muffler, set them engines up a notch . . . Drape him over that Cadillac hood."

It was not done easily. Sprocket lost a front tooth when Razor's bloody hand slipped off Ward's ankle, but it was done.

"That's Miss Frost's Caddy," Freddie yelled from the bleachers.

"Hold it, Patriots," One-Star commanded. "Move him over to that '70 Lincoln. Miss Frost is bad news."

Ward was shifted over to an older model and spread-eagled across the hood, completely exposed to the stars.

Knowing the agony he faced, Ward tried to concentrate his consciousness on one spot to blot out his physical awareness. In the irrelevancy of panic, the only positive thought he could muster came from his gratitude that the new cars had no radiator ornaments. Then, all the power of his imagination focused on the head of Chief Pontiac, two braids, hooked nose, jutting chin, but one feather or a war bonnet?

When his imagery wavered in mental confusion, Ward knew no instant yoga would soften the pain he must face, the anguish, the indignity of emasculation, but face it he would. Not for it nor what the potent Patriots in their rage might else inflict would he cry, "Hold." Sustained by indomitable hate, he would survive and return to plant the blood-avenging toe into the crotch of Big Papa, Brazos, Arms, the Barber, Breeches, Crank Case, Crotch

Job, Hoot Owl, Lefty, the Loon, Muffler, Razor and, yes, Little Mama.

What mattered sex to a eunuch?

Closing his eyes, Ward awaited the first slash from the sprocket chain of a New Right flagellant.

CHAPTER SIX

.

Concentrated on thoughts of revenge, Ward was oblivious to the hoot of an owl and the quavering of a loon, to hands releasing his limbs or the voice of Brazos speaking with quiet urgency, "The fuzz . . . Patriots, let's get outta here."

He was first conscious of a rough hand shaking his shoulder, the far-off dwindling roar of gunned hogs, and a voice of authority ordering, "Off the hood, Juliet. All your Romeos have left you."

Ward opened his eyes to see a man with a new helmet looking down at him with the old contempt. Instead of the terrifying stars and stripes, the helmet bore the emblem of the Sheriff's Department, County of Los Angeles. Weakened by shock and blood loss, Ward struggled to a sitting position as the deputy called across the lot, "I've caught their red-headed fairy over here, Sarge . . . We can book him for indecent exposure and property damage. He's messed up the hood of a Lincoln."

Before the sergeant answered, Ward heard the high-pitched voice of Freddie calling as he rounded the line of cars, "He ain't the one, Mr. Poe-leece. I'm a witness."

With incredible speed the deputy pivoted on his huge hocks, drew his pistol, and was pointing it at Freddie and yelling, "Up against the wall, you black mother-lover."

"I tell y'all, I'm the one who called the poe-leece . . ."

Without breaking the flow of his babble, Freddie turned and leaped twenty feet to land flat-footed in front of the wall behind him. While in flight his legs spread wide, and when he landed his palms were pressed against the wall, his head lowered, his butt jutting out in a stance for the frisk.

". . . I'm not going to be calling the poe-leece on myself, am I? You gentlemen done saved that young white gentleman. He didn't mess up that Lincoln, sirs . . ."

Other deputies, guns drawn, were converging on the slender black, and one was moving cautiously forward to make the frisk, using the same sidling motion of the Patriots. Freddie's whining expostulations amazed Ward. Moments before, the gazelle had talked with glibness and wit. Now he sounded like a field hand caught in the chicken house.

Crack a black with a billy club and you'll find a darky, Ward thought, and dropped his eyes to his crotch. What he saw exposed, whole and unharmed, brought tears of happiness. All he had forgone, the quiet companionship of home and Ester, the lure of the beckoning Diana, all the mountains and hillocks of love, were restored. Like the mad King Lear, he had not thought enough of these things. As his tears slowly dried, as he contemplated the marvel, a gentleness exuded through his pride of ownership and protectiveness.

"Lord of my love," he murmured, "to whom in vassalage your merit has my duty strongly knit, how much more beautiful does beauty seem when your sweet ornament before it stands. In those sessions of sweet silent thought when memory, making beautiful old loves, lifts up your burning head . . ."

Rapt in contemplation, Ward did not see the denouement of the drama against the wall, but he got the effects when he heard a deputy close by ask, "Is he praying, Sarge?"

"Maybe. Could be one of those Oriental religions that keep cropping up along Sunset."

Ward looked up at a semicircle of deputies around the hood which included Freddie, relaxed and smiling.

"Mr. Atascadero," the sergeant said, "this black gentleman has explained the situation to us. We've radioed for the meat wagon, compliments of the taxpayers, to take you to the Wilcox Receiving Hospital and get that head sewed up, compliments of the taxpayers. Your counselor, here, tells us you'll not be preferring charges . . ."

"Like hell!" Ward snapped. "Those bastards took my helmet, my wallet, and damned near scalped me."

"He's still out of his head, sir." Freddie said to the sergeant. "Don't pay him no never-mind."

Freddie didn't want him to bring charges because Freddie, as a witness, would have been in danger of retribution by the Patriots. As a public-spirited citizen, Ward would have ordinarily overridden such considerations, but there was one he couldn't overlook. Alexander Ward was a fugitive from Stanford. An investigation would uncover his identity.

"I suppose he's right, officer," Ward said. "After all, they did leave my motorcycle."

"And your family jewels," the sergeant reminded him, "which it might be advisable to cover up. Be sure to catch that ambulance. There may not be another until midnight."

Ward slid from the hood, pulling up his trousers.

After the squad cars left, Freddie steadied the wavering Ward as they walked down the alley. For Ward, the lacerations were less painful than memory of the senseless brutality he had witnessed from so intimate a viewpoint.

"Freddie, I'm getting even with the Patriots, one at a time or in a group. For my own convenience, I hope I can get them all together. That's a Stanford vow."

"Forget them. They'd kill you and get away with it. They've made a name for themselves with the Establishment at student rallies and peace parades by knocking heads. Anyhow, they're not too bad. Some gangs in Watts make the Patriots look like a sensitivity-encounter group."

Freddie's easy handling of big words brought a question from Ward. "Where'd you learn that Uncle Tom act you put on?"

"From Miss Frost. I can't beat the white power structure, but I can bend it my way."

"They really called you a mother-lover. I expected to hear something more pungent."

"It's the new breed of sheriffs," Freddie explained. "Next month they're coming at us with pink night sticks."

As they turned toward the boulevard, Ward asked bluntly, "Why are you doing all this for a whitey?"

"To save my pigeon. I figure you for *mucho* bread,

since you'll be around the Daisy Chain looking for the Greek chick."

"Forget it. I'm so broke I couldn't pass the hat-check girl bare-headed."

"I got a key to the back door. Be my guest. I work there mornings as assistant maintenance engineer to Big John, who has administrative control of all lavatories . . . Here, sit on the curb."

Ward sat. None of the barefoots milling along the sidewalk made any comments about his bloody head, but twice he heard the remark, "Dig that red suede shirt."

Far down the boulevard Ward heard an approaching siren, and suddenly he moaned. "Good heavens! I'm broke, and Big John will take my message off the board."

"I'll have him keep it on the board and put the bill on my tab," Freddie said, reaching into his jeans to pull out a five-dollar bill and a one-dollar bill. "Here's bean money."

"I can't take it, Freddie. I'm broke and out of work."

Freddie tucked the money into the pocket of Ward's black leather jacket and buttoned the flap. "You've got a job. Report to me, tomorrow night at ten-thirty, at the Kitten Club, six blocks east of here. I moonlight as Systems Analyst Expert for the Kitten Club's Traffic Placement Department. I'll deduct my twelve bucks from your pay."

"Twelve? This is only six."

"The six extra's to cover my loss of time on the job. You put me late to work . . . But don't worry about paying me back. I'm holding your motorcycle in the Daisy Chain store room as security."

"So you'll still have your pigeon?"

Edging out into the street to flag down the ambulance, Freddie said, "You're my investment, now. I figure any hog jockey with eight hundred twenty dollars in his pocket who chases a pair of teats into the middle of a motorcycle gang to get a haircut and then tries to bring charges with his pants down has too much machismo for me to let off the hook. But stash your red suede shirt when

you report for work. It'll cut down on your income . . .
Be seeing you, scabhead."

On Tuesday morning, Joe Cabroni composed a message
to be sent outside routine police channels.

From: Detective Lieutenant Joseph M. Cabroni,
          SFPD.
To: Director, Federal Bureau of Investigation.

In the course of an investigation into the disappearance of Doctor Ruth Diane Gordon, aged 72, professor emeritus of gerontology, Stanford University,
nightclub entrepreneur and owner-director of several
homes for the aged, facets of the case uncovered by
this investigator indicate areas of possible Federal
interest.

A suspect in the disappearance, Doctor Alexander
Wheeler Ward, professor of molecular biology, Stanford University, is also missing and alleged to have
fled to Mexico. Reputedly Doctor Ward was engaged
in research pointing toward reconstitution of defective DNA molecules. Doctor Gordon was an authority on the theory of random error in the aging
process which holds that aging occurs from an accumulation of defective inner cellular DNA molecules.

Nowhere in the communication did Cabroni advance
an opinion, merely editing the facts to fit his theory; but
he considered his findings important enough to teletype
his message and transmit along with it two photographs,
one he had obtained from the personnel file at Stanford
and one he had taken from the Ethan Allen yearbook of
Ward in his cadet's uniform at the age of eighteen.

Cabroni had not guessed wrong about the government's
interest. On Wednesday a figure high enough in the Defense Department to be regarded as a "reliable rumor"
by Washington newsmen invited to lunch a member of
the President's Scientific Advisory Committee high
enough in the hierarchy to be labeled an "unimpeachable
source."

After a third martini, the military man voiced a question. "Doctor, if it were possible to reconstitute innercellular DNA in the human body, what would be the result?"

"Well, General, that would depend. If the body were that of a female past menopause, you'd get a nubile, agile, and infertile young lady. If a man, he would again be subject to draft."

By Wednesday, Ward had found that the life style of a parking lot attendant differed widely from that of a university professor. Freddie had introduced him to the Kitten Club manager, who had required Ward to fill out an application for a Social Security number. Ward used the name Albert Atascadero and listed his birthplace as El Paso.

With street wisdom verging on the intuitive, Freddie reassured Ward in an area where Ward had been careful to voice no concern.

"Don't worry about being checked. All the Establshment wants is a cut of your take, and all I'll need each day is the money to keep your message on Big John's board. You can pay on the principal later."

Ward might have earned three meals a day on the job if his appearance had not been against him.

After the doctor at the receiving hospital had shaved his scalp and sewed the cuts, Ward had returned to the motel and rejuvenated his scalp. His head healed immediately, but there were still 422 stitches dangling from livid welts which made his head resemble the striped end of a hairy ape.

Traveling light, he had brought only the suede shirt Freddie had warned him against wearing. When he washed the blood out and hung it to dry, he found it, the next morning, so shrunken as to be unusable. All that was left to him in the way of a shirt was the top half of the pajamas Ester had given him for his birthday. Before checking out of the motel, he took a towel to fashion into a turban. The white silk pajamas with the Nehru collar and the turban made him resemble a swami.

His appearance caused no flap on Sunset Boulevard, but the patrons of the Kitten Club were constantly stopping him to talk about the Indian rope trick, cobra training, or Hindu philosophy. Such conversations reduced his tips. While Freddie parked cars, often as not Ward was standing under the club's canopy discussing the *Bhagavad Gita* with some tomcat or club kitten.

But he was developing his cunning. His suede shirt was so shrunken that he sold it to a filling station owner for $2.50 as a chamois cloth.

Ward's sleeping accommodations were arranged by Freddie, who gave him directions to a hippie commune near Ferndell in Griffith Park and drove him there the first night.

On their way, Ward voiced his misgivings about sleeping out in a public place, unsheltered and unprotected, with no toilet facilities.

"Look at it this way, Swami. It's like you've got one of the biggest pads in town, sixty thousand acres, airy and sunny, only an hour and a half's walk from work. Public toilets on Ferndell give you free utilities, compliments of the taxpayer. Of course, you'll have to use the restrooms before the gates open, because the cops will roust you if they find you in the park in daylight. Lay low in the ravine during the day. The hippies will feed you."

"At least I'll get to study those beasts in their natural habitat."

"They're people, Al. They'll share everything with you. Trouble is, they don't have much."

When Freddie stopped at the gate to Ferndell at the end of Western Avenue, he admonished Ward, "Keep your shirt and turban clean for the parking lot, and when you come to work, walk on a straight line. The fuzz won't stop you if you're headed somewhere, like out of town."

In the moonlight, Ward found the ravine without difficulty and stretched out with his head pillowed on his shirt wrapped in his towel. After he had removed a few pebbles from his bed, a weirdly pleasant nostalgia riffled his mind. It was his first sleep on the ground since the Battle of the Bulge, and Southern California was immensely preferable to wintry Belgium with German mortars dropping in. Though almost penniless and by now a hunted fugitive, he felt absurdly free.

"Man, where'd you get that groovy head?"

A young man, bearded, slender, wearing velvet jacket and tennis shoes without socks was looking down at him in the light of dawn. From somewhere in the ravine, Ward smelled the odor of food as he raised on one elbow.

"The haircut's compliment of the taxpayers. The grooves come from the Orange County Patriots."

"They broke Glue Head's arm at the Laguna Festival. You bring any pot?"

"Pot? I haven't even had breakfast."

"I'll tell Sadie to save you some, but don't come till I call."

Ward tried to go back to sleep, but the sun had broken through the hills and it blared into his eyes. He arose, stashed his shirt and turban in a rock crevice, and waited until the boy reappeared around a shoulder of the hills and whistled, "Okay, Baldy."

Ward followed him up the ravine. Two girls and a boy passed them coming out, all three dressed in jeans, slit serapes, and floppy hats. Compared to Ward, they were well-groomed, and he said, "Hi."

They said "Hi," and averted their eyes.

Above, they walked onto a level area hardly larger than a tennis court and overshadowed by a huge oak. A girl was stirring something in a lard pail hung over a fire of charcoal briquettes.

"That's Sadie," the boy pointed, "and she'll feed you."

The boy turned and went down the ravine. Ward walked over to his hostess, a tall, raw-boned girl whose thin face peered through a slit in her hair as she glanced at him, momentarily, then looked away.

"Good morning," he said.

"Morning," she said, motioning toward the pot. "There it is. It ain't ham and eggs, but it'll do."

She pronounced eggs as "eyeggs," and he said, "You're from the Blue Ridge Mountains."

"East Tennessee," she answered, not looking at him.

"Like it here?"

"Better than Dallas. Worse than Tampa. If you ain't got no spoon, use the big one."

Ward took the bent ladle hanging over the side of the

pot, squatted down by the fire and scraped the bottom for the remaining morsels of mulligan stew. His appetite overcame his fear of hepatitis, and he found the concoction tasty.

"Does everyone eat separately?" he asked.

"Just you. Your head ain't nice to eat with. Scrape the can. It saves cleaning."

"This is good chow, Sadie. Where'd you get it?"

"Scrounging. The bacon's store-bought."

The stew was vegetables flavored with bacon, but he said truthfully, "It tastes good, Sadie. Can I pay you something?"

"Put it in the can nailed to the tree."

"What's the charge?"

"Whatever you put in."

Ward set the pail and ladle down and walked over to the tree. Inside the can were a quarter and a dime. The two coins looked so lonely they were pathetic. He dropped in four quarters, one-fourth of last night's tips, after Freddie's deductions.

"Wow," a voice called from above, and Ward looked up to see a beardless boy with the face of a cherub framed in brown curls, shirtless and barefoot, his Levis straddling the limb of the oak.

"What are you doing up there?"

"I like trees. Do you like trees?"

"They all look alike to me."

"They're different, after you get to know them. Like this one's my old man. It digs me."

Childish enthusiasm in the boy's voice brought agreement into Ward's. "Maybe you're right. Getting and spending we lay waste our powers; nothing we see in nature that is ours."

"You talk pretty, but, man, if we get rain, I bet your head grows a crop of corn. It's plowed and sprouting already."

Ward turned back to the glen where Sadie was kicking dirt onto the charcoal and walked over to help her.

"What do you do during the day?" he asked.

"Get out of the park, mostly, so's not to pester people. Everybody but Glue Head and Nature Boy, yonder. Police don't bother them. They ain't right bright . . . Be seeing you."

Sadie scooted down the path toward the restrooms and Ward waited a moment before following, to spare her the embarrassment of his company.

His first impressions of the hippies were mixed, but their first impression of him had been uniform—he revolted them. Instead of long hair, he had stitches dangling from the lacerations made by the Barber's sprocket chain, and it took an act of courage for him to face the washroom mirror. As he plucked the stitches from his scalp, with each pull he cursed a Patriot by name. After he had run through the roster for the eighth time, Ward knew he could never return to his own age group until he had taught that segment of youth the wisdom of non-violence.

His resolution was implemented when he returned to the glade and met the other victim of the Patriots, Glue Head. Shirtless, his ribs showing through the skin of his reedy chest, the boy was sitting yogi-style under the oak, his gaze focused far beyond the hills. His hair was plaited into black braids that dangled below his sternum and his bearded face was cadaverous. The right forearm, folded across his chest, was bent from an ill-set bone.

He resembled a mystic in a deep trance, but he looked up as Ward approached and said, "Shanti. Have you got any pot?"

"Shalom. No. Am I interrupting your meditations?"

"There are no interruptions for one who is one with Manito, the great spirit, for I am one-eighth Apache, of the tribe of Sequoia."

"Manito was Algonquin," Ward commented conversationally, "and Sequoia was a Cherokee. But does marijuana help in your religious transports?"

"Man, that's where it's at," the boy said. "When I first talked to God I was sniffing glue."

"That's Glue Head, Baldy," Nature Boy called from his perch as Glue Head's eyes again drifted off focus. "He can't get his head straight. He's got more kinks in it than you've got in yours."

Ward looked around at the hills, thinking, if there was

one quick way to make contact with the commune, marijuana would be it.

Griffith Park encompassed a range of hills which would have been listed as a mountain range in Vermont. Somewhere in its gulches and canyons, Asiatic hemp might have sprouted, and he was familiar with the plant through lectures given by the San Jose Police Department.

He walked under the oak and called up into its branches, "Nature Boy, do you think you can tear yourself away from your dad long enough to help me hunt for *Cannabis sativa?*"

A floppy-brimmed felt hat dropped from the tree.

"I will if you'll wear that."

Before noon they returned from the hills with their tea harvest and tedded it on a warm boulder for further drying in the midday sun. Ward split for Hollywood Boulevard, where he bought three corncob pipes, one for him and two for the commune. He still feared hepatitis.

At twilight, Ward smoked the pipes of peace with the children of the commune, eleven boys and five girls, feeling only a mild euphoria as they talked, speaking from spheres of alienation and listening to echoes from other spheres in the rock music on their transistor radio. Rapping with them, Ward elicited few generalizations about their life style.

They were supposed to be products of affluence, but most came from families which had long been casualties in the war against poverty. They were supposed to be products of permissiveness, but all had experienced parental indifference or brutality. Since few had salable skills, they were less drop-outs from society than rejects of the economy. They were supposed to be dirty, but most of the boys worked at odd jobs as dishwashers and at auto-cleaning racks and were well washed. He had heard they were promiscuous, and he assumed the rumor was true, since it was unlikely that they should differ from other strata of society in that respect.

As had Ward when young, they sought answers to the unanswerable, but unlike him they could not even frame the questions. Still, to learn their speech patterns, he listened attentively and, finally, sympathetically.

They seemed to value his audience and began to gather around him. He caught the drift of their changing opinion in the names they called him: Baldy, at first, then Groovy Head, and, after he rigged a sleeping hammock, finally Machismo.

With slight effort he could have become patriarch of the tribe, as Sadie was its matriarch, because he was a man of purpose and their minds were like medusae, amorphous, moved by random winds, tentacles trailing for chance nutrients. As the love generation, they were as eager to give affection as to receive it, and any man of authority, personal or official, he felt, might have commanded their loyalties by appreciating their affection. But he had other purposes.

Ward could not cavil over their choice of life styles. In the summers of his own youth, before he won a scholarship, he had gone long-haired and barefooted from necessity. And if one took the inscription at the base of the Statue of Liberty literally, these boys and girls were archetypal Americans.

Actually he felt a greater affinity toward Freddie, who was also work-oriented and purposeful. Freddie planned to study law in September to "find out what laws I can bend my way."

Freddie's hang-up was the white power structure, a nebulous entity that Ward himself had fought for half his lifetime. During a lull in their parking lot activities, Ward asked Freddie what he meant by "white power structure."

"Man, I strum a mean bass fiddle in my own trio, The Untannables. But while a black artist like me's mopping floors at the Daisy Chain, Glamorgan drags down twelve hundred a week mewling over buttercups, love, and all that she-it."

Given time, Ward might have been sympathetic toward Freddie's struggle with the white power structure, but Ward was too busy hustling, and a week after the haircut, he was trapped in Freddie's black power structure.

Ward's peonage began in the parking lot.

In his turban and silk Nehru pajama top, Ward was an impressive figure, and he struck the fancy of a kitten interested in Zen Buddhism. Since she considered him her guru, she often came down during her break between eleven and midnight when the floor show was in progress to discuss Zen.

On the night of his subjection to Freddie, Ward was demonstrating a method of attaining satori to the kitten in the rear of a limousine owned by a pussy-loving evangelist from Texas which was semi-permanently parked on the lot weekdays. In the beginning of the discussion Ward heard sirens along Sunset Boulevard, a not unusual sound, and as his demonstration got under way it sounded from the street as if a four-alarm fire had broken out. He was completing the zazen of the koan when he heard from the street level above a terse order shouted at Freddie, "Up against the wall, you black mother!" and knew a police emergency existed. Los Angeles police had entered the county sheriff's territory.

"Keep low," he whispered to the girl, who was also in a somewhat precarious position professionally, and they waited, an unusually long time, until the police completed their interrogation of Freddie and drove away. The kitten skittered back to her job, and Ward noticed the tail of her costume was broken. He started to follow and warn her, when some instinct bade him remain out of sight. Moments later, Freddie backed a car into the limousine, bumped it slightly, and got out to inspect the damage.

"Keep low, guru," he whispered back to Ward. "I got some questions to ask. Have you assassinated a president?"

"You know better. With the money you pay me, I couldn't buy an air rifle."

"Is your real name Alexander Ward?"

"Yes."

"Why did you tell me it was Atascadero?"

"I didn't. You told me . . . What's this all about?"

"They got a photograph of you, old-style with hair, wearing clothes like in the Minuteman commercial. What do they want you for?"

"Murder, I think. Can you find out?"

"Maybe, but keep low. Man, it's like Bonnie and Clyde out here."

Crouched in the car and listening to the sirens, Ward knew the dragnet was for no mere murderer. Since Cabroni was using his cadet photograph, it followed that the detective had an inkling about the rejuvenation method. If Ward were caught, his youth would be a dead giveaway. It was imperative that his secret be kept as long as one gene from a Patriot was lodged among mankind's chromosomes. Humanity was not ready for immortality.

Within twenty minutes, Freddie was sidling alongside the limousine, whistling. He paused by the window.

"Here's the scoop. It's murder, man. The cops have roadblocks at every intersection between Doheny and Fairfax, and they're pulling hair, looking for a wig-wearer with welts on his head."

"My credit cards," Ward groaned.

"Right on. I called a friend on the *Free Press*. One of the Patriots was caught signing your name to an airline credit card."

"How can I get off the Strip, Freddie?"

"I can arrange it, if you'll agree to a contract."

"Let's arrange first. Any contract signed under duress is not legal."

"Did I hear you say 'legal'?" Freddie bent closer.

"I said 'legal.' "

"Couldn't hear for the sirens up there looking for you . . . I'll take your word, Al. One thing I don't want is your signature."

"What do you want?"

"Half of anything you earn while you're with me, after expenses for board and room are deducted."

"How do you expect me to hustle a buck while hiding?"

"I'll make arrangements."

"You're the damnedest person for making arrangements I've ever seen."

"Are you a racist, Al?"

"Not before I met you."

"That means you're taking my offer."

"It's the only offer I've got."

"Good. When you hear my car pull up, hop into the trunk."

Crouched on the floor, Ward waited as Freddie arranged for a substitute lot attendant. Finally, he heard the rattle of Freddie's coupé being backed alongside and the squeak of its trunk being lifted. He slithered out of the limousine, dodged across the lighted strip between cars, crawled into the trunk, and was locked into darkness companioned only by a spare tire, tools, and an empty bourbon bottle.

Freddie stopped twice on the way to their destination. Aurally alert, Ward deduced from outside sounds that the first stop was at a liquor store. He heard the clink of bottles and bemoaned Freddie's Negro irresponsibility. But at the second stop Ward remained almost half an hour in his cramped confines before he heard anything at all. When he heard a woman's footsteps approach, heard the right and left doors open and close on a murmur of voices, he cursed African eroticism aloud into the beginning roar of the transmission as his hand closed around the neck of the bourbon bottle. Freddie had stopped to pick up a date.

Later, when Ward felt the sharp turns and maneuverings to get into a parking area, knowledge of his dependency on Freddie stifled his rage. Finally, the trunk opened and he emerged, without the bottle, into the semidarkness of a garage behind an old-fashioned brick apartment house. A woman of about forty, solidly built, wearing slacks, a striped sweater, and an Afro and carrying a large handbag, stood beside Freddie, who held a sack.

"Hattie, meet Al," Freddie said to the woman, who nodded, distracted by apprehension.

"Hattie's a make-up artist at the studios, Al," Freddie said, "and she's going ahead to open my kitchen door, over yonder. As soon as it's open, you walk across and in, fast. Don't run . . . Put your Social Security card or anything that could identify you in that bumper tire nailed against the wall. That's my first rule: no papers in the house, for you or me."

Freddie was taking his own pocket book and putting it in the tire. "It will all be safe, here," he said, "because I lock the garage with a combination lock. There'll be no keys around the house, either . . . Move out."

Ward walked across the area from the line of garages to the building as Freddie pulled down the garage door, locked it, and followed. Inside, Freddie set his sack on the sink and walked down a hallway, turning on lights as he went. Behind him, Hattie followed, swaying as she walked.

They passed a bathroom on the left, a bedroom on the right, and entered a large, high-ceilinged living room with a fireplace against the wall to Ward's left and the entrance to the right in an alcove formed by the outjut of a clothes closet.

Room furnishings were Sears Roebuck modern with a television and high-fidelity combo. Freddie motioned toward the divan for Ward to be seated.

"You're on Van Ness, just south of Pico. Make yourself at home, but never answer the phone or the doorbell," he said, opening the closet door and taking out a TV table.

"You shouldn't have brought Hattie into this," Ward said. "She could get into trouble."

"Bless you, honey," the woman smiled. "I got in trouble by being born."

"She'll get a bonus for her risk," Freddie said, unfolding the TV table beside a vinyl-covered lounge chair and clicking on a floor lamp.

"Get me three clean towels, Freddie," Hattie said, opening her bag for a folded plastic smock. Ward watched her slip into the smock. All of these people were supposed to have rhythm, but Hattie composed symphonies in the twist of her hips counterpointed by the bend of her elbows. Her only discordant note was the hairdo.

As if in answer to Ward's unvoiced complaint, Hattie reached up and lifted the Afro from her head, laying it on the table. Beneath it was her own hair, glossy black. She raised both hands and fluffed it into bouffant waves in a gesture as feminine and intimate as a wriggle into panties.

"Hattie," Ward's astonishment overcame his reserve, "why do you wear that hayrick?"

"Child, I was just carrying it. That Afro's for you, honey." She chuckled at his consternation, and patted the lounger. "Now, you get out of them pajamas and come over here and lay down."

Ward felt an inswoop of his world lines around her ovals as he slipped off his pajama top and pranced to the chair.

"Lordy mercy, honey," Hattie exclaimed. "You're a virgin."

"Now, just how did you know that?"

Because Hattie seemed so proud of his innocence, he feared a negative implication might disappoint her. She made him feel like the teacher's pet, and he liked the feeling.

"You cakewalk so shy," she explained.

Freddie returned and handed Hattie the towels and set the sack on the table, removing four bottles of artificial tanning lotion.

"In the first phase of my three-phase master plan," he said to Ward, "you pass over the color line backwards. Cost of materials, six-sixty plus tax."

"For that I could buy enough tannic acid and liquid enzymes to bathe myself black all over."

"What'd I tell you, Hattie?" Freddie said. "This man's got machismo, even if he is a racist and murderer."

"Lean back on the towel, honey," Hattie said to Ward. "This boy's no racist. First thing he worried about was me."

"You're right, Hattie," Ward asserted. "Maybe I got a little racist after I met Freddie, but you've turned me all around."

"There's some tannic acid on the set I can borrow and save you from Freddie's bookkeeping . . . Now, close your eyes, honey. I got to dye your eyebrows. Freddie, start dabbing that stuff on his hands and wrists. Dab, don't rub."

She was intent on him, as if he were a piece of clay to be molded and patted into shape, and it delighted him to be treated as an object rather than as a subject.

"This lotion won't make you much more than a high yellow. I'll get you some tannin over, tomorrow, so you be thinking about what shade you want, creamy chocolate, rich brown, gleaming ebony."

"I want to be just like you, Hattie."

"Now, that's a sweet thing to say."

Impulsively she squeezed his head against her breast and Ward knew the contact was an encounter. There was more to Hattie than warmth and understanding and ovateness—she was the quintessential black mammy.

"He'll need more than skin to qualify," Freddie said. "You don't get soul by eating chitlings. I got to teach him how to walk and talk in phase two."

"He's got to learn rhythm," Hattie said. "Now, honey, these nostril expanders going to be a little uncomfortable, at first. But you'll get used to them.

"The Afro may be too big," her voice was soft and reassuring, "but your welts help and I can build up your head here and there with latex."

She pulled a rubber cap over his skull, scissored off portions she didn't need, and fitted the wig. It was snug but not uncomfortable. "It's best to be a little big to give your hair room to grow, but if a policeman grabs it, don't pull contrary . . . You can open your eyes now, baby. I brought some brown contacts so the brothers won't call you a blue-eyed devil."

"What's this third phase, Freddie?" Ward asked, sitting up as Hattie rummaged in her bag for the lenses.

Freddie thought for a moment.

"We'll talk about it when you're ready," he finally said. "I don't want you blowing your mind and splitting to Alabama."

"To Alabama?"

"That's where you come from, Mobile."

As Hattie polished and inserted the brown contact lens, it occurred to Ward that Freddie had a standard operating procedure for concealing fugitives, but why the insistence on Mobile, Alabama? Criminals did not bother with pedigrees.

"Hattie, you're the most," Freddie exploded. "He looks like Harry Bellafonte, gone mod."

"Freddie, get him a denim shirt to hide the white and that big mirror in your bedroom. I want my baby to see how pretty he is."

As soon as Freddie had cleared the room, Hattie bent low and whispered. "I'll be here in the morning with the tanning to give you the whole treatment. I'm not letting any fox spoil my baby's vine, because, honey, I dig those big brown eyes."

Except for a single barrier, becoming a Negro was not difficult for Ward after Hattie immersed him in a dilute solution of tannic acid and liquid enzymes and matched his overall color to her own. His ease at crossing the color line he attributed to Anglo-Saxon adaptability and his previous grounding in theory; he was well versed in the poetry of Paul Dunbar and the essays of James Baldwin.

On Sunday, Freddie tested him with an outing along Central Avenue, and Ward enjoyed his new peer group's informality, gusto, and mirth, which existed despite the depression of the 1930s which still lingered in the black community. Ward's verbal sensitivity demanded a substitute for Freddie's favorite expression, but he found such a wide range of speech that his expletive, "Fe-cees," was merely considered a novelty.

Their evening ended on a note that would recur. Ward and a telephone operator with an A.B. in English from Morris Brown were discussing the poetry of Winthrop Mackworth Praed when Freddie came to the booth.

"Tarbaby, we got to split. I'm busted."

They paid for their outing with a three-day diet of chili beans.

Confined as he was, Ward's life might have been tedious had it not been for Hattie's lessons in Afro rhythms given whenever Freddie's absence and her work permitted. He became adept at the Senegalese Shimmy, the Simba Crawl, and the Congo Conga, but he never learned the Springbok Spin, even though he practiced alone with two pillows.

Hattie comforted him in his failure. No white man had ever performed a Springbok Spin, she told him, but he sensed her disappointment. Nevertheless, when she and her estranged husband were about to be reconciled, she granted him an unofficial diploma after he performed a medley of Afro rhythms to a record by Thelonius Monk. The Springbok Spin was the only color barrier Ward could not break.

An old familiar dread returned to Ward in the apartment on Van Ness—poverty. Torn as he was between a growing nostalgia for Ester and his longing for Diana, the bonds that linked him to Freddie became both stronger and more galling. As household budget master, he began to wake up at Freddie's return from the parking lot to count out the parking tips on the kitchen table. A massive pile of quarters yielded only a few dollars, at times as low as seven, and the look of defeat and harassment on Freddie's face brought Ward memories of his father, counting out his W.P.A. wages with the same expression of defeat. Facing Freddie over the futile stacks of coins, Ward felt an unfocused anguish for the lad more profound than the pain he had felt from the Barber's sprocket chain.

All Freddie's talent for hustling was adequate for only one man's survival, and Ward, a prisoner of time as well as of space, was helpless to assist his companion.

As his depression deepened, Ward's loneliness grew stronger. At night, as he tossed on the couch in the living room, his hand would reach out for Ester, and unless his palm cupped the overstuffed arm rest of the sofa, he would awaken from loneliness. One night he missed the arm rest and awakened with a line from Gerard Manley Hopkins, altered by his subconscious, ringing in his mind:

"Ester are you grieving over Alexander's leaving?"

Immediately he was wide awake, thinking of Glamorgan and his theft from Wyatt. If the Welsh Bard relished antiquity, then that idle singer of empty lays might be a market for more "original" song lyrics.

Rubbing his eyes, Ward staggered into the midnight kitchen, tore a sheet from the roll of paper towels, took a pencil from the cupboard drawer, and sat down to write an updated version of Hopkins's "Spring and Fall." Though driven by needs that mocked mere honesty, Ward was hag-ridden by the self-reproach as he twisted the poet's lines, yet, in the manner of a poet writing porno for profit, he generated a peculiar enthusiasm for the work. When finished, he realized that "Mini-Boppers and Swingers," though inspired by the loss of Ester, had the off-beat charm, the mixture of antiquity and modernity Diana Aphrodite had projected that afternoon in his laboratory.

When Freddie came in from the parking lot at 2:30, Ward showed him the lyrics and explained his plan. Tired and worried, Freddie merely glanced at the composition.

"It might be a good song, Al, but I can't hustle Glamorgan. Like it's artistic integrity. I'm a bass fiddle virtuoso and old Baby's Bottom can't fret a three-string lute."

Pulling his hand from his pocket, Freddie poured a trickle of coins onto the table top, and a glance told Ward there was less than a day's rent.

"Old buddy," Freddie said, "I didn't want to start phase three so soon, but we need bread. I got you an appointment for a job in the Daisy Chain, out of sight. You'll have to pass the missy, and if you can pass with her you can pass in the Congo."

"The missy?"

"Miss Frost. Big John and I call her the missy to humor her. She's old-timey in her thinking. She's an old lady, and that's the way she was raised."

Freddie slumped onto the sofa, worried and preoccupied, and Ward sat across from him, thinking.

At the Daisy Chain he could meet Glamorgan, and no artistic integrity prevented Ward from pitching his lyrics; but man did not live by bread alone. Little Mama was an habitué of the discotheque, and he could use Dolores to lure the Patriots to him; and blood had a ritual value. There, too, the still silent Diana would seek him.

"One thing, Al," Freddie sounded embarrassed, "don't pull your cakewalk strut around the missy, and keep your voice respectful. If you get to sign an application, don't dash off your signature like a bank president. Write slowly, keeping your eyes about five inches from the paper, and squint."

"Are you telling me to put on a plantation shuffle?"

"I know how you feel about black pride, Al, but the missy expects things."

"I don't buy this servility bit," Ward snapped. "It hurts the black image."

"What's being polite, man?" Freddie flared. "Are you servile when you open a door for a chick, or help her into her coat, or take off your hat? Miss Frost is quality folks. She's strict, but she's fair."

Ward caught himself. Freddie had been instructing him in nothing more than old-fashioned courtesy, and he had become so involved in the black ambience that he was hypersensitive to race.

"Don't worry, Freddie. I'll be happy to talk to the phantom of the Daisy Chain."

"She's for real, man, but she has to be seen to be believed. And nobody talks to Miss Frost. The appointment's for her to talk to you. All you say is 'Yes'm' and 'Thanky ma'am.'"

CHAPTER SEVEN

.

Freddie parked behind the Daisy Chain, unlocked the rear door, and led Ward in. Inside, they wound up narrow iron stairs spiraling around a steel pole, past the bird cage, past the machinery for its lift, upward into shadows, and across a catwalk to a door. Past the door, they entered a white-on-white reception lobby, carpeted in white, with two white Louis XVI chairs and a table below a long mirror. Before them were an elevator door, a door to their right, and a door to the left.

"Miss Frost's private elevator," Freddie whispered, pointing. "Miss Frost's private john . . . Miss Frost's telephone number is unlisted."

Ward stifled an impulse to take off his shoes as Freddie turned to the door on their left and rapped lightly.

Inside, a voice tinkled like sleigh bells. "Come in, Freddie. You're three minutes early."

Freddie opened the door and entered, saying, "Excuse me for interrupting, Missy, but I brought the new man, Al Atascadero."

Entering, Ward saw a trim body, precise in its movements, turn from a white filing cabinet at their entrance and stride across a white carpet to a white desk in the center of the room.

Ward had never seen a person so aptly named as Miss Frost. In her mid-forties, young for Ward, though old for Freddie, she was as remote and as beautiful as a distant snow peak rising above white clouds. Her eyes were gray, her skin pale, her hair a silvery gray tinged with the blue of glaciers. As she crossed to her desk, he glimpsed an elegance of legs hosed in silvered mist beneath an off-white tailored miniskirt. The vision of her legs was reassuring to a man with fears of breast obsession.

110

She swung behind her desk and stood to appraise the new arrival with a formal but not unfriendly glance. Before her the desk was bare except for a white pen in a white holder, a white telephone to her left, and on her right, on a white pillow, a white Pomeranian. The dog growled softly and bared its teeth, but Ward's eyes were all for Miss Frost. So regal she seemed taller than her five feet, she was an immaculancy of white against the white Louis Seize paneling of the office, which reminded him of an 18th-century Big John's john.

Before he caught her accent or her scent, some radar acquired with his new pigmentation told him she was a Southerner.

"Atascadero? Unusual name for a Nigra. Your old folks back home must have been owned by Spanish Creoles."

"Yes'm. We come from Mobile."

"A very good stock in that region. Some Masai blood with an infusion of Nubian. I know your area well, Al, for we are fellow Alabamans."

"Thanky, ma'am."

Then Miss Frost smiled at him and her smile was as elegant as her legs, as imperious as her stride, and Ward knew that Miss Frost was not merely a Southerner—she was a Southern Aristocrat, no doubt, descended in a straight line from some wealthy family of slave traders. And she was the quintessential white missy.

"So, you think you might be interested in a maintenance engineering job at the Electric Daisy Chain? Very good. I like to see ambition in colored folks. But I must warn you I'm a strict taskmistress. As Freddie can tell you, I tolerate no Stepin Fetchits at the Electric Daisy Chain. We expect an honest hour's work for our dollar and a quarter's pay."

It was the first mention of salary. Since it was twenty cents under the legal minimum and Freddie would get half of it, Ward would have preferred less title and more pay. But to mention money would have been an affront to the truly august presence.

"I work hard, ma'am."

"I will make that decision, Al . . . Now, step over

yonder and fetch me the white manila folder." She pointed.

In his eagerness Ward pranced over and pranced back, and he knew his prancing had been a tactical error. Despite Freddie's warning, he had forgotten to shuffle. Strange lights glittered in her eyes, and her voice grew harsh.

"Lay it there."

She pointed to a spot on the desk in front of her and he complied.

"Pull up that chair."

She pointed to a chair against the wall with an un-painted wicker bottom, the only non-white area in the room. Moving aside the Louis Seize chair before her desk, Ward brought the wicker chair.

When he returned, Miss Frost was seated behind her desk, her arched back pivoted forward on her pelvis, leafing through the folder.

"Sit!"

He sat. She pulled an application from the folder and a ballpoint pen from the desk, turned the form to face Ward, laid the pen atop the form, and handed them across the desk to Ward, who took them. The dog growled sleepily at his movement.

"Fill in your Social Security number, here, and sign your name, here."

Ward took his Social Security card from his denim jumper, wrote the number slowly on the line designated, and began, laboriously, to spell out his name.

"I declare, it shouldn't take forever to sign your name."

"I don't write good, ma'am."

"Go home tonight and practice. Write your name at least fifty times, you hear?"

"Yes'm."

"Not that I approve of too much education . . . Oh, well. Return the chair."

Ward returned the chair and turned back to stand before her.

No longer smiling, Miss Frost looked up at him and through him as if he were standing far behind him-self.

"You are now a member of the Electric Daisy Chain Maintenance Engineering Staff. You will be directly responsible to Freddie, who is directly responsible to Big John, who is Chief Maintenance Engineer. Always keep in mind, if you tote the water with dispatch and swing the mop with efficiency, you may someday rise to Big John's position. Dismissed."

"Thanky, ma'am."

Walking softly, they left her office and vestibule, tripped down the stairs, and ran onto the main ballroom floor, swapping African handslaps.

"Man, you made it," Freddie chortled. "She's got the hots for you. I saw it when you gave her that little do-si-do cakewalk."

"How do you figure?" Ward asked. "She got hostile."

"When she starts looking mean, that's because she hates herself for what she's wanting. Missy was raised in Alabama. Someday, she's going to rise and overcome her raising, and the missy's day of atonement's going to be some black man's day of jubilee. Man, it could be you, and I want a raise in pay when you're up there influencing policy. Whooee!"

Freddie was fantasizing, but his insight into the cause of Miss Frost's sudden hostility might be beautiful and true. In a manner Freddie had not foreseen, Miss Frost had blown Ward's mind with a vision of her flashing legs.

Two dollars a day of a debt that had been accumulating for eighteen days was wiped out when Freddie re-introduced Ward to his new boss, Big John. At the introduction, Ward threw Big John a rhyme to put the old man in a good frame of mind.

"You're a good rhymer, I have to admit, but you're not the champion wit." Big John pointed toward Ward's message on top of his board. "I keep that message as a monument to a young hog jockey who came and went. He got no answer from the lass, but the boy was a master of classical gas."

Looking at Freddie, Ward said to Big John, "I regret I'm not tops, but I'll holler you no hollers, for you just saved me thirty-six dollars."

Outside, as they went to get mop buckets and mops,

Freddie explained the thirty-six dollars he had put on Ward's tab.

"Man, getting something for nothing ruins your character."

An attempt to obtain thirty-six dollars by fraud from a victim under duress was not exactly character-building for Freddie, either, but in Ward's continuing dialogue with the young, Freddie was a captive audience who could be taught honesty. There was a greater con artist on the premises—Glamorgan, whose audience was more immediately desired by Ward for economic reasons. And after Glamorgan, the Orange County Patriots.

Perhaps from contriteness, more probably because he knew Ward was hooked by Miss Frost, Freddie gave Ward the keys to the motorcycle at the end of their half-day.

"You may as well drive it, man. You're into me so far, now, the motorcycle won't start to recoup my losses if you split."

Ward encountered strange barriers in his first attempts to speak to Glamorgan. The Welsh Bard rehearsed every morning, except Sundays, between ten and eleven-fifteen in the ballroom of the Electric Daisy Chain. In his retinue from Europe were his sound engineer, his arranger, his director, and his hairdresser. All hummed around the artist, dragging wires on their earphones over Ward's floor, putting sneaker marks on still-damp places, zooming in to get a better view of Glamorgan's profile, back-pedaling for a fuller view of his figure.

Freddie split the scene when the group were rehearsing, leaving the floor and its cleaning to his assistant. Though the troupe were polite to Ward, they regarded him as an animate object.

"You, there. Would you move your buckets back a bit? Thenk yo."

They were focused on Glamorgan.

"Lift your voice just a decibel, Glam, on 'lo-ove' to give the audience the full flavor of your Welsh lilt. Wonderful. Now, you register perfectly."

"Glamorgan, I don't think you're sad enough to sing

'Blue Mists' tonight. Let's match your mood with 'Little Buttercup.'"

Even Glamorgan's spontaneity was rehearsed.

"When you turn your head," his director said, "let's give them your bright instead of your tender smile, to set the stage for 'Little Buttercup.' As you turn, twist your head a little more briskly and let's flip that right curl over your shoulder . . . Now, try again . . . Henry, there's something wrong with that flipping curl."

And Henry would trip forward to finger a ringlet. "Oh, dear, I've dreadfully overdone the spray. Half a mo, Gorgeous One, and we'll have your locks springing again."

Ward understood Freddie's shyness in this company. Glamorgan's retainers were expert at the Establishment Shuffle. But Ward was from the Establishment, himself, and as he mopped he waited for a breach in the wall.

Three days after his first day at work, Ward spotted an opening. During a coffee break, he heard Glamorgan say, "What I wouldn't give for a spot of well-brewed tea."

On the fourth morning just before the coffee break Ward sidled brashly into the group, saying, "Mr. Glamorgan, being as you're from England, I expect you'd like a cup of fresh-brewed tea about now."

"Indeed I would, my good man, but I'm from Wales."

Minutes later, when Ward returned from the store room hot plate with cups, tea, sugar and cream, a slice of lemon in a bowl, and napkins, he was the focus of British gratitude.

"Tell me, fellow, what is your name?"

The question came from the great Glamorgan, himself, and Ward knew his year of graduate work at Oxford had not been in vain. There he had learned to brew tea, English style.

"Jest Al, sir. Jest Al."

From that moment on, Jest Al became the favorite American of this wandering contingent of alleged Welshmen.

Teatime became Ward's second favorite period at the Electric Daisy Chain. His first favorite time came when the whine of the elevator told him Miss Frost was coming down to look in on the rehearsals.

At such times, Ward's mop adopted a new tempo and he pranced behind it, swishing closer to the spot where she invariably stood. Sometimes a bright "Good morning" tinkled out of the shadows, but out of her voice's range he could still see her, dressed in white, a most adorable and gracious ghost.

Never once did she criticize his floor work, and his imagination took flight in her presence. She was Helen on the ramparts of Troy looking out over the camps of the Greeks where a black Hector fought in her defense. She was Dido without a willow in her hand wafting her love, Othello, to come again to Carthage. And from her, always, his nostrils picked up the perfume of magnolias fresh-bloomed by moonlight.

Since she barely touched a demure thirty-eight, she was his proof that he was not breast-obsessed.

On the first Monday after the beginning of the tea breaks, Ward brought the typed lyrics of the song he had titled "Mini-Boppers and Swingers" for a reading by the Welsh Bard. Perhaps as a joke, Glamorgan held his hand up for silence, set down his tea, and said, "Listen to these words from Jest Al."

> Ester were you grieving
> When you heard my cycle leaving?
> Warm, like the love of man, you
> In your innocence care for, can you?
> But as his fires bank lower
> Boy comes to bedroll slower.
>
> No matter, Ester, how you slice it,
> Love's a game with loaded dice. It
> Can't be won but only played.
> All innocents into earth are laid.
> Knowing then what you were born for,
> Is it virtue that you mourn for?

When Glamorgan finished, there was a dead silence from his group, and his classical brow puckered. In admiration, or disgust? Ward wondered as he waited.

In reproach.

"Ester's spelled with an 'h,'" Glamorgan said.

Ward's Ester never used the "h" because no one pronounced it.

"She's a Cockney, Mr. Glamorgan. This song was written just for you."

"Just 'Glamorgan,' please. And I'm not a Cockney . . . But the lines do have a pretty sentiment."

"Sentiment, man," Ward exploded. "It's the real Mc-Kuen. Look at the sprung rhythms. You don't see them, any more. And get a load of that mixed metaphor in the middle."

Glamorgan was studying the script.

"You do talk rather strangely, Jest Al, even for a black . . . Pardon me, old man. I mean you'd talk strangely even if you were white . . . Ah, yes. I see. How does one slice a dice game? Rather odd, but amusing. Why don't we use 'Mary'? That's an honest name."

Glamorgan must have had a hang-up on a girl named Mary, Ward decided, but, more important, his use of the word "we" indicated an interest in the lyrics.

"Mary's just fine," Ward said. "And a name like that won't distract from the sentiment."

"Or even Margaret," Glamorgan was lost in thought. "I had a bird in Liver . . . Cardiff, once, named . . ."

"Not Margaret," Ward interjected. "I caught clap in Cleveland once from a girl called herself 'Margaret.'"

"Oh, very well!" A bit of Liverpool whine invaded the Welsh lilt. Ward sensed he was in for a put-down, but negotiations had begun and Ward had deliberately written flaws into the lines to ease negotiations.

"How much do you want for this thing, as it stands?"

"Whatever you think it's worth, sir," Ward said. "Say, about two hundred bucks?"

"That's more than this mucking dive pays me in a week."

If Freddie had told the truth, the statement was either a thousand-dollar lie or the masterful bit of British understatement. But Ward, back-pedaling in sympathy, delivered a low blow.

"Man, that's no bread in Birkenhead."

"What do you know about Birkenhead?"

"Nothing," Ward parried. "Just a Big John rhyming joke."

"You are the peculiar one . . . Al, I'm willing to record the song and advance you fifty dollars against ten percent of the royalties. Is that fair?"

"That's fifty percent fair on the advance, but only twenty-five percent fair on the royalties."

"But I'm the artist," Glamorgan jabbed.

"I'm the poet," Ward jabbed back.

"It's *my* name that draws. I compose the tune and play it. Playing sprung rhythms on a three-stringed lute demands skill. And the lyrics will have to be changed, old boy."

Glamorgan had dropped his guard. Ward's face froze in hurt and hostility.

"Sorry. I meant 'old chap.'" Glamorgan was contrite.

"Half of that money goes to the AA2CP," Ward said.

From the ropes, Glamorgan asked, "Is that something like Snick?"

"That's me and my roomie. Our rent's due . . . But what's this about changing the lyrics?"

Still on the defensive, Glamorgan was glad to get back to specifics. "This line, 'All innocents into earth are laid,' won't come off. I suggest 'All maidens are eventually laid' to give the lyrics an upbeat ending for mini-bopper virgins."

Ward had rehearsed his answer. "That'd be all right for nightclubs, sir, but it would get you banned on radio."

Puckering his brows, the Welsh Bard said thoughtfully, "And praps telly."

It was a masterful maneuver. As Ward was translating the remark into "And perhaps television," the Welsh Bard struck.

"Jest Al, you're too bloody materialistic for a poet. I'll go one hundred dollars against forty percent of the royalties."

Negotiations were ended, but Ward hedged. "That's fine, as long as you put my name Jest Al on the label."

"Good, I'll have my manager draw up the contract . . . But why not your entire name? Are you on the lam?"

Ward nodded. "Aggravated assault in Mobile. I broke a musician's guitar over his head because he welshed on a deal . . . Beg pardon. Because he went back on a deal."

"You felon." Glamorgan smiled his bright smile as he pulled out a roll of bills. "Well, one confidence deserves another. I was rapped once with a statutory, myself, in Liverpool."

Two nights later, Glamorgan sang "Youth Grows Wiser," the ultimately agreed-upon title, to a whistling, whooping, foot-stamping ovation which had not stopped after four encores when Glamorgan carried on the remainder of his program. The next day, the Welsh Bard cut a 45 r.p.m. which the recording company air-expressed to its distributors. Within the week, "Youth Grows Wiser" had knocked a Johnny Cash from first place and had set the development of country and Western rock back by six weeks.

Glamorgan wanted more Jest Al lyrics, so he pushed for and got an early royalty payment which the company advanced on forecasts. Ward split his proceeds with Freddie, paid Freddie $449 back room and board plus services, sent Ester $1,000, tithed $280 in the poor box of Our Lady of the Angels to the memory of Gerard Manley Hopkins, and had enough left over for a wild weekend in Watts.

Thereafter money accumulated so fast he opened a checking account at a Western Avenue bank under the name A. Ward and halved with Freddie by check. Now cash stilled Ward's conscience as he went plucking lyrics from the public domain. Poe's "To Helen," retitled "To Hattie," disappointed him, but Burns's "Whistle and I'll Come, My Love" almost upset Hopkins. The Silky Sullivan in the pop lyrics field was Winthrop Mackworth Praed, 1802–1839, who held seventh place for six weeks and then jumped to second, hanging there for two weeks, then moving ahead of Wilde's "The Ballad of Folsom Jail" which had, by then, edged out Hopkins.

But the listings were tabulated later. Ward spent the remainder of June swabbing floors, writing lyrics, looking for Dolores, and waiting for an answer to Dionysus's message from Aphrodite. Diana's failure to respond shadowed his triumphs with anxiety.

Next to her desecration, he feared Diana's death. If she died, he would be consigned forever to youth and darkness, becoming, as it were, the Wandering Negro.

By the end of July, Freddie had bought a lavender Cadillac with his half of the royalties, and he became thenceforward Freddie the High Wheeler. While monitoring a new song by Glamorgan, Ward also met Margie again and found that Miss Frost had banned Dolores from the premises. She was too controversial, politically.

The climax of July came when Glamorgan refused to accept another extension at the Daisy Chain and accepted an offer to appear in Las Vegas for twenty grand a week.

At news of Glamorgan's departure, Ward arranged with the record company to send a fourth of the music royalties to Ester. Actually, the giant step upward on the salary scale was a relief to Ward, who was overloaded with cash and welcomed a chance to lay by the Welsh Bard's lute.

The new attraction at the Daisy Chain was Gollenberger and Stein, specialists in songs with a social message. They were in rehearsal two weeks before Glamorgan's departure, and Ward's maintenance work suffered. In soprano voices, the duet wailed discords about lonely lampposts, littered streets, forlorn garbage pails, and children leaning out of windows for love. Sometimes, between songs, they wept over their own keenings and their sorrows warped the orbit of Ward's mop because he sympathized with despair.

Having heard of Jest Al, the Mop-Handle Poet, Gollenberger and Stein shyly let it be known that they would like a few of Ward's lyrics if he could work in social content. Ward liked them although they were liberals and, as a black, white liberals turned him off. But Gollenberger and Stein had "schmaltz," the Jewish equivalent of "soul," and both had natural Afros.

He might have converted "The Love Song of J. Alfred Prufrock" into their style of protest music, but T. S. Eliot was not in the public domain. The 18th-century poets were lacking in social consciousness. In addition, he was too tired—tired of his job, tired of waiting, tired of writing.

An encounter with Miss Frost near the end of the week's hiatus between Glamorgan's final performance and the Gollenberger and Stein opening night pointed up to Ward the degree of his weariness.

On that morning he was swishing his mop two-thirds of the way from the bandstand to the edge of the dance floor, while unseen in the shadows Miss Frost was watching. Despite the high notes from the musicians at their final rehearsal, he ordinarily would have heard her elevator, smelled her, or sensed her through more basic vibration.

Suddenly she spoke from behind him.

"Al, you're giving that floor nothing but a lick and a promise. If you keep this up, you'll be reduced to a janitor."

Her voice was snappish and without a trace of that furtive longing which Freddie called "the hots." Looking toward the bandstand lights, he could tell from the reflection on the floor that she was right.

"Yes'm."

"I declare, you've been mooning ever since Glamorgan left. Are you some sex degenerate? Is it Glamorgan that you moon for?"

"No'm."

"Look at that mop. It's not even wrung out properly. Fetch me the mop bucket."

He hurried across the floor at her command and she called after him, "You've even lost your prance."

After he returned with the bucket, she put the mop in the wringer, hoisted her skirt, and lifted her leg to press down on the wringer pedal.

"That's how it's done." She brandished the dry mop in front of him. "Now, you do that whole area over again, you lazy no-'count, and put enough grits in your gizzard to write a nice song for those Jewish boys, unless you're one of those anti-Semitic Nigras as well as a pervert. That pap they're whining is entirely too negative for the Electric Daisy Chain. You write them a song about happy darkies, you hear?"

"Yes'm."

Hands on her hips, she looked at him with something approaching contempt. "Dionysus, indeed. Hmmph."

She turned and strode from him, heading toward her private elevator, as he wondered vaguely how she knew that he was Dionysus. Then another thought came to him, bringing with it overpowering evidence of his decline.

When the silver flash of Miss Frost's inner thigh had glimmered in the glow from the bandstand, he had been no more interested in Miss Frost's legs than he would have been interested in the legs of a jaybird.

Ward motorcycled home that afternoon on a hog his caution had turned to a piglet and walked into the apartment to sit heavily on the divan. Freddie entered and handed him a copy of the *Los Angeles Times* folded back to the fourth page.

"Is this your old man?"

Ward was looking at a one-column cut of himself made from a wedding portrait he had had taken with Ester.

FUGITIVE TOUTED
FOR NOBEL AWARD

Doctor Alexander Ward, biology professor at Stanford University, sought for questioning since early June in the disappearance and suspected murder of Doctor Ruth Gordon, Stanford gerontologist and financier, was listed among nominees for the Nobel Prize, Friday. Doctor Ward's contribution was a system of analysis which extends mathematical reasoning to include organic reactions.

According to Doctor Sir Peter Waverly-Pritchard, visiting professor of theoretical mathematics at Stanford, Doctor Ward's system opens the way to include organic phenomena in the Unified Field Theory.

Ward disliked "touted" for "nominated" in a story on the Nobel awards, although he supposed headline writers had to watch character count. But Freddie had asked him a question.

"Yes," Ward answered.

"Murder must run in your family . . . I'm taking a nap. Would you give me a call about six?"

"Better set the alarm, Freddie. I'm dead myself."

"Okay, but burn that paper."

Ward went to the fireplace and burned the paper, thinking, even my brain's tired. His ideas had been irrelevant, detached. The big story was his own nomination for the Nobel Prize, which meant he should have no trouble getting his grant extended on his terms.

No. He was a fugitive from justice, and the big story was that Ruth Gordon was a financier. With good reason he had always assumed she was poverty-stricken, but even if she had money to carry out experiments in human biological controls, she still did not have him, the missing link . . . linkage.

Getting back to the divan was an uphill effort. Galloping anemia? he wondered. There was so much he had to think about, and the most he could do was remember the afternoon in the patio and someone talking about a C note set on a tuning fork. Disassociated linkage?

Ward slept to awaken dully at the sound of Freddie's alarm clock, dozed, and reawakened when Freddie slammed the kitchen door, going out in his "poor" clothes to hustle tips at the parking lot. Ward wondered why Freddie continued the work. Now that he was a Cadillac owner, he was parking cars so cautiously his tips were halved. Still, the parking lot was a listening post. Recently Freddie had brought news that both Army and Navy Intelligence had joined in the hunt for Ward.

When he heard Freddie's car go out the driveway, Ward went to the garage to get his solution and electrodes. He felt rested, but he lacked the inward fire that composing songs demanded, and the missy had asked him to write a song about happy darkies. He would have to work a little social protest into the happiness for Gollenberger and Stein and a few acoustic patterns for himself.

Ward had no theory about his fatigue, only a vague hunch. But when he stepped from the bath to towel himself and caught himself whistling as he scrubbed, his hunch had advanced to a hypothesis. He swung into the kitchen, tore a paper towel from the roll, and sat at the table with his favorite pencil stub. Before starting to write the song, he scribbled out the master equation for molecular disintegration he planned to use as the theme of his lyrics and set it to one side.

He bent to write.

It was then Ward wrote the last and crowning lyrics of Jest Al's career in words as pristine as if newly coined from the sweat, tears, and tumult of black fate. At the outset it was all there, hopelessness, frustration, rejection, rage, jingling in Negritic rhythms from his memories of Saturday nights in Watts. Yet into his words came also a wine-dark laughter.

He was writing the immortal "Flutter High, Butterfly."

In the artlessness of genius, Ward knew not what he wrought. Essentially he was trying to construct an acoustics pattern matching a series of dissonant high notes to appropriate vocal sounds. Thus the simplicity and originality of his opening lines, so seldom sung but so essential to the *motif* of the entire poem:

> Swinging through the alleys wild,
>   Jiving sounds of rhythmic glee,
> On a fence I saw a child
>   And he, laughing, said to me,
>   "Daddy-O, make a song for me."

The child symbolizes the primitive savage and thus, by extension, the oppressed proletariat of the world, whereas "Daddy-O," as an exuberant cognomen, relates the child more closely to Rousseau's version of the primitive as a noble savage and expresses the artist's faith in the irrepressible good humor of the common man. As a symbol, the central figure, or Daddy-O himself, extends beyond Rousseau, back to the chthonian roots of myth, and is more appropriately represented, perhaps, as Prometheus bringing fire (laughter) to the world.

But the critical appraisals would come later.

Certainly, seated at the table, one eye closed, six inches away from the paper, Ward could not foresee that in a matter of a fortnight his words would be whanging out in Mandarin among the rice-wine bars of Canton and clicking in Swahili through the cantinas of Mozambique.

> Flutter high, butterfly,
> High, high into the sky.
> That bright disk of sun afire you
> Cannot reach but can aspire to.

He was not conscious that he was writing a masterpiece, but after Gollenberger and Stein's opening night he knew the sounds had a functional effectiveness that no one could understand besides him and Doctor Sir Peter Waverly-Pritchard in Palo Alto.

Two nights later Ward sat with Freddie, front row center, weary from muscle fatigue. He had worked overtime waxing the ballroom floor for the opening.

At first, Gollenberger and Stein's musical appeals to social consciousness were lost on an audience of boys and girls who came mostly from Beverly Hills and Bel Aire. They found it hard to sympathize with children leaning out of windows for love while their psychiatrists were attempting to solve their own problems of alienation.

When Stein announced the finale as a new offering by Jest Al, the applause was a tribute Ward shared with Glamorgan, he knew, but the voices dropped around him. As he had planned, there was a complete silence when Stein announced that the Mop-Handle Poet wished to dedicate the number to Miss Frost. Had the woman far above them in the darkness stiffened in horror at his presumption or melted in delight at his homage? No matter. The crowd was silenced.

With Gollenberger handling the drums, Stein's voice was too high-pitched to belt out the prologue. Instead, it whiplashed against a wall of audience indifference. When it grooved into the chorus, the listeners leaned forward and the wall came tumbling down.

In a devil's mask with dry-gourd rattle, bare feet strumming a tom-tom beat, Mumbo Jumbo danced into the Daisy Chain in visions woven on pot-smoke gloom. Through the fetid smells of a jungle night, lean blacks stalked lithe black girls by their anklet clicks of leopards' teeth. A leap and cry in the velvet dark was followed by the rattle of the Simba Swap in simulated cannibal rites as the drums cried "More" to the guitar's "Stop." After the whirr of a Springbok Spin, the music circled in a cakewalk strut till dawn broke over the Congo, silvering the black, wide river.

Up from the reeds margining the banks a butterfly fluttered toward the rising sun.

Shaken, the listeners sat for a moment in silence, then began to pound the floor with their heels, begging for an encore. Though Ward's innercellular structure had been ripped by a sonic storm, his mind was rested. He had written a song about happy darkies as the missy had requested.

After the tumult died and Freddie had complimented him on their new hit, Ward said, "I reckon Miss Frost will have us waxing again tomorrow. This heel-pounding has ruined my floor."

"Man, this is no time to talk about waxing floors . . . You talk tired. Want me to drive you home?"

"No. You got to go to work. I'll make it."

Motorcycling home, Ward was revived by the night air. He knew, now, what had caused his torpor, and he knew, too, if Miss Frost didn't take him off the floor tomorrow and into the penthouse with her, he would have to resign. There was only enough solution for one more revival of his SA$^{(2)}$ factor. If she didn't take him tomorrow, she wouldn't want him after another barrage of Gollenberger and Stein's high notes.

And the Daisy Chain was the only place where Diana could find him.

At the apartment Ward brought his electrodes and solution in from the garage, but he was too tired to take a bath. Slipping into his pajama bottoms, he went into the living room to watch television, and he had hardly settled into his chair when a knock came at the door.

He went to open the door, turning on the entrance light.

Outside the screen stood two white men, crew-cut, wearing blue suits. An animal wariness about them reminded him of Joe Cabroni, which was explained when the man nearest the door held up a billfold opened to his identification and said, "We're from the FBI and we'd like to speak to Freddie the Hustler."

Despite his weariness, Ward inwardly alerted. Their information was dated; Freddie was now the High Wheeler. As the information registered on his consciousness, Ward noticed that the second man was studying his head with the same objectivity Ward had observed in the Barber and Hattie.

His best offense was no offense at all, Ward decided as he fumbled at the latch, smiling. "Why, I've seen you gentlemen on TV. Y'all come right in. Freddie will be home, directly. I'm just visiting."

Returning his billfold to his coat pocket but keeping his hand inside his coat, the first man brushed past Ward, moving quickly into the living room, saying, "Front room clear, Culpepper."

The second man entered more leisurely, saying, "This is mighty obliging of you, Uncle."

He audibly inhaled as he entered, and Ward assumed he was sniffing for marijuana. Ward, too, inhaled, and caught the unmistakable under odor of delta mud. The second agent, Culpepper, was from Mississippi. Culpepper's origins put an entirely new interpretation on his sniffing and explained the study he had made of Ward's face.

"Mind if we look over the apartment, Uncle?" He spoke with Old South courtliness as the first agent was already down the hall, leaping past the darkened bedroom door and reaching in to switch on the light.

"Y'all go right ahead, sir," Ward answered.

Ward walked slowly back to his chair, knowing now that fate had singled him out to put on the greatest Plantation Shuffle in the history of put-ons.

Culpepper was a Negro expert for the FBI.

CHAPTER EIGHT

.

Mentally Ward followed the agents through the apartment. They would find no documents to question because there were no papers in the house and no garage key. Again it occurred to Ward that Freddie's foresight was no spin-off from his sidewalk cunning. Unless Freddie had researched methods for hiding felons, this operation had been masterminded by an expert in concealment, probably someone in the nature of a financier who pretended to subsist on a widow's mite.

But Ward had dirtied the immaculate plan by leaving his electrodes in the bathroom. All that could save him, now, was his own guile.

He was thinking hard.

Interservice rivalry was two-edged. Cabroni could have concealed the part that electrodes played in the rejuvenation process in hope of scoring a coup, himself, ahead of the FBI, LAPD and ONI. Ward had decided to bluff on that assumption when the Northerner came into the living room holding the electrodes.

"What are these for?"

"Them's my de-magnetizers, sir."

"How do they work?"

Culpepper had entered and was listening.

"You plug them in and hold one in one hand and one in the other, facing east. Chiropractor tells me that magnetism stuff comes from the north. Electricity coming from the south churns up your blood. They help tired blood, and I had tired blood since I been born."

"Sickle cell anemia, Cabot," Culpepper explained. "Lots of them have it."

As Cabot returned the electrodes to the bathroom, Culpepper brought the three-way lamp closer to the chair, turning it higher, and pulled a picture of Freddie from his pocket.

"Is this Freddie?"

"Yes, sir. That's old Freddie. He wanted by the FBI?"

"Only for questioning, Uncle, about this man."

Culpepper flipped the picture and on the back was the Ethan Allen portrait of Ward. "Ever see him?"

"Yes, sir. I saw him around here, or somebody who looks a lot like him."

As Ward studied the photograph, he knew Culpepper was studying him under the bright light.

"Does he pick up his mail here?"

So the post office had been the source of their information. They had traced Ester's royalty checks back to the publisher or record company and gotten the address from there.

"Can't say he does, sir. He shaves sometimes. Maybe takes a bath."

"Does he have a blue streak down his back?"

"I don't recollect looking."

Cabot had returned, and Culpepper explained. "They can pass for white with their clothes on, but the blue streak down their spine is a dead giveaway."

Culpepper took the photographs and replaced the floor lamp, saying, "You've been a help, Uncle. Now, we'll just sit here and watch television with you until Freddie gets back."

After they were seated on the divan Ward knew he was still undergoing an in-depth analysis by the Southerner, even though he had passed the physical.

"What kind of shows do you like best, Uncle?"

"I reckon I like them war pictures best, sir." . . . With you whities killing each other.

"How about cowboys and Indians?"

"Can't rightly say I likes them, sir." . . . That's too close to home, Mr. FBI.

"What about those sexy modern movies, Uncle?" . . . With all those white girls getting toosed into the hay?

"Whooeee!"

"Where do you hail from, Uncle?"

It was a loaded question designed to lead to regional

allusions about the South, and Ward, nodding sleepily, diverted Culpepper with a decoy in a rambling answer.

"Compton, sir. Got freewayed out when they put in that new freeway between the Harbor and the Santa Ana. Can't find a new place. With ten cents family assistance and twenty-cent rent, man sleeps he can't eat, eats he can't sleep."

Culpepper let him ramble on about the happy problems of happy people until Cabot interjected, "Have you been questioned by the Los Angeles police?"

"No, sir. Nobody talk to me but you gentlemen."

Ward could hear the divan springs creak as the agent relaxed in relief.

But Culpepper was back, tugging, with Ward anticipating the direction of his pull.

"How are you related to Freddie, Uncle?"

"Now, lemme think . . . My mama's youngest sister, that's Aunt Delphi, she married Uncle Henry. He's a good Christian when he's sober. His sister, my Aunt Emaline by marriage . . ."

In the time-honored manner of the South, Ward traced the relationship through a labyrinth as Culpepper listened respectfully, but the Northerner, Cabot, grew impatient with Southern amenities.

"We've been here half an hour and you said he'd be back directly. When is 'directly'? "

"Bout two o'clock in the morning. Sometimes three, when there's a big turnout after the last show."

"They have a careless sense of time," Culpepper explained.

"I don't have," Cabot snapped. He was through with Culpepper's explanations.

"Are you telling me Freddie's at work?" He asked Ward.

"Yes, sir. He runs the parking lot at the Kitten Club."

"I know where it is," Cabot said. "We can be there in twenty minutes. Let's go."

Culpepper arose, asking, "Do you have a telephone, Uncle?"

"Yes, sir. Right there in the hall."

"Don't use it," he said, and his voice was harsh and

authoritative, the voice of the Man. "If Freddie's gone when we get there, we'll know you called him and that's aiding and abetting. Then we'll be back, and you won't have any rent problem for a long time."

"Yes, sir."

As they went out the door, Ward heard Culpepper explain to Cabot, "He's an old-time darky. He'll do as he's told."

But Ward was already getting up to turn off the TV set when he heard the squeal of rubber going north; he dashed into the bathroom to turn on the water and rig his electrodes. While the water was running, he stepped into the hall and called Freddie.

A strangely composed Freddie listened as Ward explained what had happened. When he answered, his voice was reassuring.

"They can't do anything to me if I don't know where you are, and I won't know by the time they get here . . . Listen, in ten minutes, call 696–9000. Don't call sooner, for I'll have the line tied up. You'll get instructions from there. Good luck, old buddy. And remember to leave a check for my half of our bank account."

Ten minutes were all Ward needed for the rejuvenation bath using his last ounce of sugar phosphate and adding the tanning and enzymes for a combined operation that left him young and blacker. The tanning seemed to speed up the rejuvenation.

On the evidence of the telephone number, Ward knew that Freddie was not a free-lance conductor on an underground railway. Perhaps a division superintendent would answer his call, but Ruth Gordon had switched him onto this side track, for only Ruth Gordon would have charged $449 for two weeks' room, board, and expenses.

Naked in the hallway, he dialed the number Freddie had given and heard a tinkle of falling icicles in the answering "Hello."

"Miss Frost! Freddie give me your private number."

"Of course, Al. He tells me you're in a little trouble with the law. Never fear. The Electric Daisy Chain provides for its key personnel. Have you pencil and paper?"

"Yes'm," Ward lied, thinking it strange she didn't know

such articles were contraband around the apartment. But then her voice was as patronizing as ever. Miss Frost truly thought of him as a black, which meant she was merely a strand in the net of conspiracy.

"Hop on your bike and take the Santa Monica Freeway west to the very end. Keep on 101, past Malibu Village, and turn right at Vertigo Čanyon Drive. Don't turn left. There's an ocean out there. Follow Vertigo to Rattlesnake Junction, then make a sharp left on Canyon Diablo. Follow Diablo until you reach Paseo de la Muerte and follow it north until it dead-ends on Fiend's Crest Road. Follow Fiend's Crest left until you reach a barrier, with reflectors. Don't drive through it. There's a three-hundred-foot drop beyond into Lost Indian Canyon. To the right you'll see a private gravel road skirting the face of a cliff. Follow the road over Dead Prospector's Saddleback as it winds around a pasture atop the plateau, curving toward Satan's Summit. Atop the crag you'll see a ranch house that's headquarters for the Adorable U Beauty Ranch. The porch light will be on. Go right up to the front door, knock, and don't gape at whoever answers . . . Got that?"

"Yes'm."

"And, Al, I do wish to thank you for that lovely dedication. Your song was so . . . sensual."

Her bells were twanging deeper notes, but Ward had no time for romance.

"Who do I ask for, ma'am, when I get there?"

"Miss Diana . . . Miss Diana Aphrodite."

He thanked her and hung up.

Despite the energy Ward put into dressing for the road, a pall was hanging over his mind which lingered as he dashed to the garage to get his checkbook from the spare tire. Miss Frost's directions had been a verbal chamber of horrors over-draped with the black anapest, Malibu; "Mal," Latin for evil, "ibu," Javanese for "place of spirits." Malibu, the place of evil spirits.

Extrapolating from his last two bank statements, Ward wrote out a check for $121,287.44, Freddie's half of all he had earned while under Freddie's care, and laid the

check on the kitchen sink. Then he headed for the garage
and his motorcycle.

Heading west at 11:15 on a Saturday night before the
bars let out, Ward had the Santa Monica Freeway to himself. At eighty miles an hour, slowing for 101, he took only
twenty minutes to reach the Vertigo Canyon turn-off and
headed north into the Santa Monica Mountains. At Rattlesnake Junction, Canyon Diablo demanded careful driving
to negotiate its curves, but it was just a warm-up for Paseo
de la Muerte. The latter road twisted through a narrow
canyon, uphill all the way, with only a streak of stars
above to remind Ward that a universe existed. He was
genuinely relieved to break out onto Fiend's Crest into the
full light of the stars and a half moon low in the west.

Turning west on a road without habitations, he drove
carefully along rock-imbedded asphalt. Yellow eyes of
wild things glared from scrub lining the road, and once a
deer bounded across ahead of him. Finally he reached the
barrier. Off to the right he found the gravel-paved shelf
that wound above Lost Indian Canyon. To negotiate the
abyss in the dark, he pushed the motorcycle the quarter-
mile to Dead Prospector's Saddleback before remounting
to putt-putt slowly down across the meadow.

Off to the west, outlined by the gibbous moon, he saw
a ranch house atop a rocky knoll. Huge, dark, and for-
bidding, the building loomed above Satan's Summit, and
the road made a wide half-circle below, the bight of its
U traversing a stand of eucalyptus, as if the road were
wary of the house. Breaking from the trees to approach
from the north, Ward saw a faint light marking the
entrance. It was well that Miss Frost had not requested
that he enter by the rear door. Built in the form of a T,
the two-storied structure's rear wing extended so far south
the journey to its back door would have challenged a goat
in daylight.

Drawing closer, he saw the west facade was canti-
levered from the knoll to form a carport with a sub-level
apartment, possibly a bunkhouse or chauffeur's quarters,
adjoining a freight elevator and loading platform. One

automobile, a white Porsche, was parked in the garage adjoining the stairway to the entrance.

Not only the car was Diana's, but the entire ranch house, Ward realized, after he had parked and was mounting the stairs. The lower veranda, extending the width of the fifty-yard structure, was lighted by a single entrance light, a forty-watt bulb.

So, inside the house the girl of some of his dreams awaited, and he was not happy. With such resources, Ruth Gordon, alias Diana Aphrodite, had kept him waiting in poverty, hounded by police, while she plotted to halt evolution before human beings had evolved from savagery.

Mindful of Miss Frost's warning not to gape at who opened the door, Ward pushed the doorbell and waited, bracing when he heard the doorknob turn. Framed in the lighted hallway was a diminutive competitor of Ester, dressed in a black, miniskirted maid's uniform cut low above a lacy white apron. A heart-shaped doily topped her mass of chestnut curls.

"*Entre, s'il vous plais.*"

Entering, Ward bent low in his plantation bow and in response she curtsied. Her torso had the shape of a champagne glass, and at the bottom of his bow he sniffed her bouquet. When she straightened from her curtsy, her bowl almost bubbled over, and Ward felt that in another era she would have been from Louis XIV's private vintage at the Petit Trianon.

"*Vous etre senegales.*" She spoke from astonishment.

If she wanted a Senegalese, his duty and his desire were clear.

"*Oui'm, j'est senegalese,*" he answered in plantation French.

"Was madame expecting . . ." she started to say, and remembered her manners. "Please, come with me to the library."

Prancing, Ward followed her behind, catching in his side vision lithographs of Picassos and Modiglianis in plastic frames on plywood walls stained to resemble oak panels. The reception hall's Woolworth–Sunset Boulevard opulence oppressed him with the parsimony he had once admired as thrift. Even Ruth's French maid was not an import. In the dip of his bow Ward had detected, subtly blended into the French smell, the tannic tang of Louisiana swamp water.

The maid was less a domestic than a trick to set him prancing. Ruth planned to put him down for his breast obsession, and all she needed for the put-down, to establish her moral superiority, was a prance. But the new Ward was hip.

At the intersection of the corridors, the maid stopped before a white double door marked "Library" in gold letters and knocked. Ward glanced about. East and south, the corridors stretched interminably, but the west hallway was closed near at hand by a temporary partition and a door marked "DO NOT ENTER."

As they waited, Ward glanced at a bulletin board to the right of the library doors.

MONDAY 3 P.M. LOWER EAST DINING HALL E-41, former professor of English, will lecture on "Trends in Modern Literature." Following the lecture, S-37, formerly tragedienne with Fanchon and Marco, will give selected readings from *The Story of O* and *The Voyeur.*

Those readings should be interesting, Ward thought, but he wondered about the tragedienne. Fanchon and Marco had been a vaudeville circuit, closed these many years. And security must be tight when a vaudeville tragedienne was not called by her name.

Suddenly both doors began to open slowly, inward.

The opening had been done for dramatic effect, and it was effective. Halfway the length of an office the size of a squash court, Diana was revealed, seated behind a desk of silver on a carpet of gold. In front of her desk was a golden chair. All around, the walls were shelved to the ceiling with books bound in white with gold lettering on their spines. Above her down-bent head, a silver chandelier cast reflections in her hair as if the very light were amorous of her curls. On her left, two golden princess telephones were placed. Before her lay a pad containing figures.

Without looking up, Diana—Ward could not think of this glory as Ruth—said, "That will be all, E-24. And you may enter, Al."

Her voice rustled as softly as wind in willows.

As the maid turned and departed down the east corridor, Ward entered slowly to a cadence counted in his mind. Giving him the busy executive ploy at midnight, Diana kept her head to a list of figures on the pad, but he knew she was peeking at his feet, waiting to see him prance.

Suddenly, she looked up at his dark skin, his Afro, and his brown eyes. "Who are you?"

"Alfred Atascadero, ma'am."

All the sounds of summer were gone from her voice. "Would you stand there, one moment?"

She was reaching for a telephone, and he translated her request as "Don't sit on my golden chair."

Apparently the phone was direct to the Daisy Chain, for she didn't dial. "Miss Frost, Miss Aphrodite. You've sent me the wrong Negro. This one doesn't speak in iambs, and he has no prance . . . Cute little shuffle! What do I care about cute little shuffles? No, I can't use this man . . . Get that black scatologist on the conference line . . . Big John, what's this all about? This man isn't Alexander Ward . . . Freddie said! I don't care what Freddie said. He lied. I paid him three hundred forty dollars for harboring one of his criminal friends. Quit rhyming at me . . ."

She was fighting to control herself, and Ward underwent a similar struggle at her remark about the $340. Ward could appreciate Freddie bilking a whitey, but his black brother had charged him $449 for the same service.

Listening, he could almost interpolate the remarks at the other end of the line.

"Big John, I try to be broadminded on matters of race, but that black scalawag tempts me. Fire him . . . I don't care if he is pining to be resigning, fire him first . . . And, Miss Frost, send a form letter to every listed sub-

scriber to the Fair Employment Code blackballing that
young man with every employer in Southern California
. . . You get it from the local FEPC office. Where else?
And, Big John, I want another message on your board,
lettered very clearly:

DIONYSUS, MY BREASTS ARE BARED.
CALL 696-9000

"Miss Frost, I don't care if every fairy in Hollywood
does call your number, I've got to find that man within
two weeks . . . I don't care if the message is obscene,
Big John, he's a breast man and that's the only lure for
the pervert . . . Suggestions. What am I going to do with
the one I've got?"

She was being a good executive now, listening to her
department heads, jotting notes, and Ward knew his fate
was being settled. A prance would reveal him, but she
had kept him up tight for over two months, and he wished
to return the favor. Besides, he could get a more rounded
view of her methodology from the bottom, and there were
a few areas of investigation he wished to explore in secret,
beginning tonight.

"He can saw a log or wheel a hog," she was saying,
obviously to Big John. "Well, I might use a messenger
boy . . . Dodge a cop or swing a mop. Well, I could use
a clean-up man . . . Good with books, brooms, and bal-
lads?"

Her face glowed at the alliteration of the three "b's,"
and Ward sensed a master psychologist at the other end
of the line.

"But I don't want him in the library . . . He's a better
man at brewing tea than any man you ever did see? How
is he on hot chocolate? . . . What were you paying him,
Miss Frost? . . . No wonder the Electric Daisy Chain's
Profit Profile was weak for July. Well, I'll correct that
here."

She hung up and looked up at the waiting Ward.

"You seem to be popular with Miss Frost, Big John,
and the police. What do the police want you for?"

"Rape, ma'am."

"In California? Come now, Al."

"No'm. In Alabama. They's old-timey back there. But I was innocent."

"No matter. Fortunately, the girls at the Adorable U Beauty Ranch are rape-proof. Are you good at running a vacuum cleaner?"

"I do my best, ma'am."

"We have a few minor cleaning chores. Guests attend their own rooms as part of our fitness course, but many aren't diligent, and I insist on dust-free rooms and spot-less baths. So you must dust all corridors and dining rooms, mop all kitchens, and clean behind each guest. At present I have only 244 occupied rooms, with more opening when the thirty-eights arrive, Wednesday. But the new arrivals will be in the lower west wing, which you must never enter. Is that understood?"

"Yes, ma'am."

"You may call me 'Miss Diana,' " she said, reaching into her desk for a key. " 'Ma'am' makes me feel ancient . . . You'll be quartered in the garage room, below, next to the elevator shaft. Your hours are from 6:30 a.m. to 12:30 p.m. at one dollar an hour plus room and board."

"That's a mite low, Miss Diana."

"Of course you may refuse my offer." She laid the key in front of him. "I'm sure the police can find you another position, at much longer hours and much less pay."

Ward picked up the key.

"Good," she said, rubbing her hands briskly together. "It's twenty minutes till your quitting time. Run down to the east-wing kitchen and prepare me a cup of choco-late. Busy, busy, I'll be working here until two."

Turning to go, Ward left behind him all idealism and devotion he had known as a youth in Dormitory C, Ethan Allen Prep. He had seen her divested of all beguilement, and Ruth Gordon was a ruthless Gorgon.

So, one adapted, he thought, checking off the room numbers as he passed; E-18, on his right, E-20, E-22. Counting on the confraternity of kitchen help, he paused at E-24 and rapped softly, hoping to get information from scullery gossip.

"*Entrez-vous,*" a voice called.

E-24 was stretched on the coverlet of her bed, reading by a 40-watt bedlamp. Her shortie nightgown was of pink chiffon much like the one Ester had modeled for him. At his entrance, E-24 lifted to one elbow to see over her breasts and asked, "*Oui?*"

"Ma'am, Miss Diana wants me to fix her some chocolate, and I was wondering if you'd be kind enough to show me where to find the makings."

"*Ma robe de chambre, garçon.*" She pointed to the closet.

At her movement, her nightgown shifted slightly and he glimpsed a swash of chestnut amid the swirl of pink, colors that set him prancing. He tripped toward the closet, his nostrils catching fumes from his own tannin. Later he analyzed, memories of swamp water engendered by his musk must have thrown her into a fit of nostalgia, for when he turned to offer her the robe, he heard a thump, a wriggle, and a swish. She had dropped her book on the floor with her nightgown atop it and lay down before him *sans habillement.*

"*Allons, garçon.*"

Ward slipped, and fell into a velvet washing machine with a spin-dry attachment. A slow Kittibangi was spurred by her "*Vite*" into a Mambo Samba, but still she whispered, "*Profonde.*"

Ward had plumbed his rather conventional depth unless he could use the principle of the inclined plane, a literal screw, as it were, and the method for exerting such leverage was not in his repertoire. But now was the moment or never at all.

Crossing one arm over, he teetered in the bight, took the breast bounce cleanly, and flung himself counterclockwise to spin in the gyre. Before he had completed the first quadrant of the full circle, Ward knew he was launching himself into history with a flawlessly executed Springbok Spin.

He alone savored the moment in its fullness, but just before she fainted E-24 breathed, "*Merci, mon bête noir.*"

Now for the kitchen and Miss Diana's chocolate.

Pouring and stirring to the recipe given him on Pinyon Verde Lane, Ward considered his night's adventure from other than historical angles. Before he closed the door, he had glanced at the title, lettered in gold on white, of the book E-24 was reading, *The Queen of Palermo's Ass—A Study of Female Sexual Aberrations.* If the little Cajun read such works, she could speak English better than she spoke French, and it was little wonder that Diana was keeping him out of the library. Whatever other elements Ruth-Diana's experiment might include, something carnal was afoot.

As a handy man for the six days following his first interview, Ward learned much.

All the guests at the ranch were young, fit, and beautiful, unlikely candidates for a health and beauty spa. Mornings they took calisthenics and interpretive dancing to the piped music of Beethoven, Brahms, and Bach on the broad sweep of lawn before the ranch house. Afternoons were spent in charm classes, and evenings were spent in the study of erotica, to the subdued music of Brahms, Beethoven, and Bach. Most were superb cooks, he discovered, because meals were prepared by the guests working in shifts and served with a flair in five dining halls. Their housekeeping skills made his job as clean-up man hardly more than that of a room inspector and gave him an opportunity to make some unusual acquaintances. E-44 was not merely a stunning girl, she also shared an interest with Ward in Etruscan art.

His room inspections tipped him to their study of erotica. Beside each bed was a well-thumbed copy of the 1924 edition of *Psychopathia Sexualis.* Krafft-Ebing was to the Adorable U Beauty Ranch what Blackstone was to the Inns of Court.

Sweeping corridors was literally a joy ride for Ward, since he rode a self-propelled vacuum sweeper. Miss Diana made no attempts to economize on labor-saving devices, apparently to cut down on the cost of help. To expedite his response when she called, she equipped Ward with a walkie-talkie.

The high degree of professionalism in so many areas by women so young led Ward to postulate a theory which was confirmed on Wednesday with the arrival of the

thirty-eights. They came in four mini-busses. Most walked
with canes, a few were wheeled out to the elevator lift,
and all were very old. On the side of each bus was
lettered:

DOCTOR GORDON'S RETIREMENT HOME
FOR LADIES

Ward counted the new arrivals as the elevator lifted
them into the forbidden west wing. Inside, he knew, the
last of his solution would be poured into bathtubs wired
with electrodes and the random errors of the aging process
would be erased.

He knew it was the last of his rejuvenation solution
because there were thirty-six old ladies, not thirty-eight.
But Ruth Gordon's control group would be complete,
the last section ready for indoctrination, and the first step
would be taken toward the eventual extinction of the
human species.

Unless he stopped her.

Meanwhile Ward was growing paler, his blackness
merging into a rich dark tan which he kept uniform by
local applications of tea leaves.

But it was not his color that betrayed him.

At ten p.m., Friday, he was vacuuming the carpet in
the lower south corridor when his walkie-talkie buzzed.

"Al, prepare me a cup of chocolate without delay and
bring it straight to the library without stopping en route."

"Wilco, Miss Diana. Out."

Her specific instructions regarding delays told him
that this was not a casual call. He levered up the vacuum
snout and gunned the sweeper down the corridor, full
speed to the kitchen. In a matter of minutes, he was plac-
ing a cup of hot chocolate and a napkin before her.

His prescience was verified when she motioned for him
to take a seat on the golden chair as she slowly sipped her
chocolate. When he had seated himself, she placed the
cup on the saucer, dabbed her lips with the napkin, and
said, "The late Doctor Ruth Gordon would have loved
the way you make chocolate."

"Thank you, Miss Diana."

"I called you here, Al, to discuss your position in relation to the library. Around us you see the second largest collection of erotica in the United States. The largest is owned by a housewife in Georgia."

"They got pretty covers, Miss Diana."

"You can learn a lot in a library," she said reflectively, leaning back. "For instance, I use a form of the Dewey Decimal System in assigning rooms to my guests. Have you noticed how my system works?"

"No, Miss Diana."

"To keep jealousy at a minimum and avoid cat fights, guests are grouped according to bust sizes. In the east wing, for instance, farthest down, I have two forty-fours, three forty-threes, five forty-twos. Then, there is E-24, merely a forty but otherwise so petite she would be, in proportion to a woman of normal height, at least a forty-four. So much for the guests."

She paused and took another appreciative sip of chocolate before continuing.

"In this library are forty volumes relating to Africa." She reached into her drawer and pulled out a stack of book cards. "They range from ceremonies, pubertal, through rites, fertility, and worship, phallic. It's no coincidence when my eleven champions have checked out among them thirty-three of those forty volumes, particularly when only three volumes per guest are permitted out at one time."

Suddenly she got up and walked around her desk toward him, flipping the edges of the cards with her thumb. She leaned back against the front of the desk, looking down at him.

"One needn't be Sherlock Holmes to deduce there's an African in the east wing."

She tapped the cards into alignment and laid them on the corner of her desk. Half leaning toward him, she spoke, and the voice once so precise with authority had softened, become feminine, and was again slumberous with the sounds of summer.

"Al, I understand your needs, but, as a woman, I ask you to understand mine. I'm old, much older than you think. When I was young it seemed youth would last forever. Then, suddenly one day, my husband was gone, my friends had all left me, and my body had grown infirm."

She reached out and stroked his cheek with the back of her hand in a movement so gentle he could not harden himself against her touch. He even enjoyed the caress.

"But there was a youth I knew when I was young and he was very young. He stayed beside me as we both grew older, and he was a bridge to my own youth. With a peculiar duality of the sacred and profane, we loved each other. But the boy adored huge breasts. All I could offer him was harmony of line, and that boy was no Euclid."

Reaching out, she cupped his chin with her free hand, and despite his knowledge of her materialism and avarice he was touched by her tragedy. No matter how much wealth she might amass, she would never have enough.

"My young love," she continued, "judged a woman's character by the distance of her dug from her sternum. A horrible obsession, but so unique it marked him as surely as his fingerprints."

On an upstroke of her hands, she had grasped his sideburns and pulled them back. Deftly she jerked off his Afro, snarling, "You dirty trickster . . . And I thought you were my old friend."

Turning, she flung his wig into the wastepaper basket and leaned against the side of her desk, sobbing. Unseen, he slipped out his nostril expanders, shucked his brown contact lenses, and rising dropped them into the basket with his wig.

Having no defense against a weeping woman, Ward moved behind her as he had the first time in her kitchen, depending on the nostalgia factor to help him back into her graces, such as they were. But the pressure of his arms around her only made her sob harder.

"Tit for tat," he said, "and I hope the expression doesn't offend you. My old friend framed me, left me broke, homeless, and hounded by the police."

"That's not true." She broke away from his embrace, flung herself around the corner of her desk, and sat down. Outraged innocence shone in her eyes, and vehemence rang in her voice. "You were under my protection from the moment you reported to Big John. I framed you to tear you away from your mother's surrogate's breasts, and I kept you under cover to keep your from mucking up my experiment with your theories . . . Did you know your hair was wavy?"

"My head's dented," he said.

She reached into her drawer and pulled out a comb, tossing it across the desk. "Sit down and comb that mop. One of my rejuves was a man's hair stylist. I'll send her up to the penthouse in the morning to trim your hair."

"Why the penthouse?" he asked, feeling absurd pleasure in combing his hair.

"You're going under the covers again, but this time with me, until you can scrub off your tan." Her tears were drying fast. "I don't want the guests to think I've taken my houseboy as a business partner, especially a houseboy with your reputation . . . I'll drive over to Westwood tomorrow and pick you up some decent clothes and an auburn wig. I prefer auburn-haired men."

"What are we partners in?"

"The Al-Diana Rest Homes for Elderly Ladies. Alex, we can make millions."

She was using the wrong approach on a man with over a hundred thousand dollars in his checking account and a Nobel Prize awaiting him in his middle age, but Ward merely said, "You can't make millions in nursing home fees."

Diana shook her head emphatically.

"Most of my patients are wealthy widows with expenses paid under estate endowment plans which take care of all their pre-need needs. As long as the widow survives, the nursing home is locked into her estate, in this case, indefinitely, for fifty dollars a day, plus expenses."

"But won't the next of kin get impatient at such longevity?"

"The relatives merely sit and wait while we take advantage of the 'plus expenses' clause. These beauty ranch courses cost $150 per day, plus expenses." Her eyes glittered and her voice rose. "From this base, we establish an international organization. What Tiger Balm did in the Orient, what Hadacol did in Louisiana, Aphrodite's Youth Juice will do in the world."

Ward didn't think the trade name very dignified, though it should be easy to remember. However, her plan posed another problem. "Estate trustees might object to beauty and fitness programs for very old ladies."

"In three months it won't matter," she said, "because the secret will be out and there's nothing illegal about rejuvenation. But this is not merely a beauty ranch. This is a staff college for the shock troops of love. We offer courses on the principles of applied romance within the framework of the free enterprise system. Practical erotic techniques are analyzed. Pelvic rhythms are developed through interpretive dancing."

She leaned forward, her body tensing with zeal. "On Labor Day, I unleash my rejuves against the fertile nubiles, pitting skill and experience against mere enthusiasm. But I'm not ignoring cultural values. These most tender moments in the memories of young lovers will be forever linked, through the background music, with the art of Beethoven, Brahms, and Bach."

"How are you arranging this classical orgy?"

"Surely I don't detect a note of disapproval in a lad with this record." She tapped the library cards on her desk.

Ward thought for a moment.

"I do disapprove of hard-core orgies, but not one with social, cultural, or artistic values."

As he commented, Diana was drawing an artist's lay-out from her center drawer to pass over to him. "One of my guests was an advertising agency artist, and she drew this up at my direction. It will run full-page in the underground newspapers."

In a border of entertwined nudes were the headlines:

Make a Date Over Labor Day
for
THE GREAT MALIBU LOVE-IN
Beethoven and Free Beer
Brahms with Beauts
Bach with Boff

Ward considered the ad.

Love-ins were passé; now it was rock festivals. Girls were no longer called "beauts," and Brahms, Beethoven, and Bach were out with the "in" generation. Diana had no knowledge of the young and apparently less empathy.

She needed several managers—an ad manager, a program manager, and a grounds foreman to prepare the pasture beneath the grove for the occasion—and all would have to be recruited long before Labor Day.

As he weighed the experiment, Ward felt the same inchoate striving toward form he had felt in his laboratory which had led him to the Theory of Universal Affinities. Ruth had an idea, here. With it, he could set up a rock festival historical in its scientific significance. And as a spin-off from the experiment he could blister Freddie for his dishonesty and burn the Patriots for their sadism.

"I'll help you with the experiment, Diana. If it succeeds, we'll start from there."

Now he could see the affinity between her plan and his.

CHAPTER NINE

Ward's loss in salary at his conditional acceptance of partnership with Diana was almost made up in fringe benefits. After moving him into her penthouse suite and office under his new cover name, "Mr. Alexander," she went to Westwood the next morning and bought him an entire wardrobe, an auburn wig, and a set of ear plugs he requested to mute her humming of pop music. But she retained title to all he wore, vexing him with such remarks as "You're handsome in my new pajamas."

In the conventional sense, Diana was not a mad scientist, merely a free-lance oddball who had used gerontology to make money. Her acquisitiveness he attributed to the Great Depression, her heritage of Yankee thrift, and her thirty-year marriage to a college professor. She was cramming possessions into a psychic vaginal hiatus; in contrast, his breast obsession qualified him as an all-American boy. Yet, Ward, by accepting her defects of character and concentrating on her physical assets, managed to love her by the Gestalt method.

She was efficient. She recruited an ad manager, program director, and grounds foreman without a penny's outlay. Mr. Alexander was appointed to all three positions by his senior partner. So, between frequent scrub baths to rid himself of tannin, Ward spent his two days in seclusion rewriting her ad, reviewing her program, and planning the layout of the grounds for the festival, but not without clashes over policy.

Their second breakfast together in the penthouse was the scene of their first domestic tiff.

To restrict the audience to the elite of the youth subculture, Diana had priced tickets at $15 for boys and $30 for girls. In a value judgment typical of her gen-

147

eration, she equated the elite of the young with the wealthy, but this "elite," Ward knew, would be drug-pushers, rock musicians, Bel Aire burglars, high-priced groupies, and UCLA sociology majors.

She wanted a predominantly male audience accompanied by girls of such proportions their escorts would pay twice for their company, or two or more escorts would split the ticket cost for shares in their company. Diana wanted only top competition matched against the girls of Adorable U.

"At these prices," Ward commented, "we'd better cancel the free beer. A full can of beer is a deadly weapon. When the crowd finds out that Beethoven, Brahms, and Bach are not a rock trio, they'll throw things."

"Cancel the beer," she said promptly, "but my recital stays. By creating an optimal environment for music appreciation, I intend to blow their minds with Beethoven, Brahms, and Bach."

"They'll wreck your grand piano," Ward insisted.

"You don't get the scene, Alex. At the prelude to Brahms's *Fourth*, the rejuves emerge from golden pavilions on each side of the stage dressed in see-through gowns of Arcadian shepherdesses . . . We'll let E-24 lead the counterclockwise procession. She sets you spinning, *mais oui?* . . . Then, E-44 leads the clockwise procession . . . You dig her, eh, Alex?"

Her asides were delivered with jealous astringency and to divert her, he remarked, "Save the forties and over for the end of the procession. We don't want a premature climax."

She ignored his suggestion, saying, "As they circle through the crowd, tossing daisies from their baskets . . ."

"Make that poppies, for symbolic value."

"They wend slowly back into the tents." She was not ignoring him but gripped by her vision. "Then, Beethoven. Tripping out to the strains of the *Eroica*, they'll be dressed in miniskirts with breakaway panties . . . You'll teach them your tantalizing little prance, won't you, Alex? . . . And Beethoven will have gripped the audience.

"Now, Bach, and the girls emerge to the grand finale of Bach's *Passion*, buxom, beautiful, and in the buff. For every lad in the audience, from that moment onward, Brahms, Beethoven, and Bach will have written 'our song.'"

Rapt in contemplation, she paused. Ward had spotted a flaw in her timing but withheld comment as he rued his inadequate musical education. Never had he suspected that Brahms, Beethoven, and Bach were concupiscent composers.

"Still, Diana, we'll need an audience, and the classics don't draw. We'll need a couple of big names in the rock field."

"Gollenberger and Stein," she said. "I don't care for their bleeding-heart social messages, but they're under contract to the Electric Daisy Chain and I'll order them here."

"They'll be excellent to back up your recital, but, musically, Gollenberger and Stein are one name. We'll need a preliminary combo to entertain early arrivals while you're getting ready."

"Forget it," she snapped. "My budget won't support paid musicians."

"Diana, we're talking of gate receipts that might hit a hundred thousand dollars."

"But I'm using the Electric Daisy Chain guards at the admissions gate. Those chiselers charge double time for holiday work."

"Then, deduct the musicians' cost from my half."

"Your *half?*" Her face froze with hostility. "By Labor Day, I'll have worked on this experiment for three months, you for three weeks. You get no half."

"From my prorated share, then."

"Policy has been decided, Alex. As a loyal member of the management team, it's your duty to implement that policy . . . Unless you're attempting a take-over of the organization."

From her remark, he gathered his pro rata would not pay for one hunched-over guitar picker, but he persisted.

"This policy hamstrings both your advertising and programming departments. To show faith, I'll get you the most sought-after trio in town for the cost, to you, of a toll call to Los Angeles."

She held up her hand for silence, thinking. He thought she would ask the name of the trio, but she said, "Very well. Since you're program director, I'll grant you telephone privileges—for this."

In the office Ward dialed, and Freddie's voice, thick with sleep, answered his greeting. "Man, you oughtn't waste your one call on me. I'm no lawyer yet."

"I'm not in jail, Freddie. Dad and I are running a booking agency for musicians."

"You two sell Murder, Incorporated?"

"Listen. Less my ten percent, I can offer your trio a one-shot booking for five hundred bucks, before an audience of five thousand, and I hear Elvis will be there, scouting for a back-up trio of blacks. How long will it take you to round up the Untannables?"

"About three days."

"Move fast. You'll only have about three weeks to rehearse, and Mr. Alexander, the program director, is a hard man to please. Choose about six modern numbers and submit your repertoire to him at ten o'clock, Labor Day morning. He'll provide lunch, but he'll want to listen to your numbers before the program starts and iron out your rough spots. Now, to get there . . ."

By the evening of the second day in the penthouse, Ward presented the rewritten ad, retaining the border and adding a map of the location, for Diana's approval.

Labor Day
THE GREAT MALIBU LOVE FESTIVAL
Groovy Groupies for All
At 2 p.m.
Introducing
Freddie the High Wheeler's
Trio
THE UNTANNABLES
(Direct from Watts)
"Music to Smoke By"

———————

Starring
Diana Aphrodite's

THE IMMORTAL DEAD TRIO
Brahms, Beethoven & Bach
(From Germany)
"Music to Stroke By"

Featuring
GOLLENBERGER & STEIN
Playing
"Flutter High, Butterfly"
(Direct from the Electric Daisy Chain)
"Music to Fly High By"

On the morning of the third day, Ward descended, lily-white beneath his auburn curls and dressed with but a single flaw to conform to the image of a rising young junior executive. Tucked under his cuffless trousers were boots. He told Diana he wore the boots to remind himself he was now a pragmatist with both feet solidly on the ground.

As one of Diana's key personnel he was given a key to the east wing, but the door was no longer locked. Rejuvenation of the thirty-eights had been completed except for hair dyes and dental work the DNA had not effected.

On motorcycle and afoot, Ward scouted the grounds, planning for himself and for the festival. Below the eucalyptus grove which formed an acoustic wall, a meadow sloped gently into a natural amphitheater for over a hundred yards to a precipitous ravine. He decided to place the acoustic shell's back to the cliff, facing the ranch house a quarter of a mile away.

In his first morning's exploration, he traversed the grove on his motorcycle several times, driving slowly among the huge boles. By noon, he was back in the office, organizing work parties.

Among the ranch guests, practically every masculine job skill was represented, for this was the generation of Rosie the Riveter. In the name of physical fitness, they dug ditches, laid pipe, did carpentry, grading, painting, and wiring for the amplifiers he spotted with mathematical precision around the perimeter of the amphitheater. Outfitted in brown, wearing pith helmets, they might whistle as he passed, but they worked.

Busy with the indoctrination of the thirty-eights, Diana signed his requisitions automatically. Miniature grading machines, wheelbarrows, gravel, lumber, and pick-up trucks were brought in from Santa Monica. Equipment was charged to the expense accounts of the guests, and it was capital equipment visible to the eye, an asset belonging to her, and not, like salaries, money gone forever.

On each side of the slowly rising stage and pink acoustic shell, golden pyramidal tents were reared on wooden floors. Inside they were air-conditioned, and pennants floated from their peaks. From exit and entrance ramps of the pavilions, white gravel walkways formed a huge peace symbol over grass growing green from the sprinkler system Ward installed. Above the amphitheater, in the shadow of the eucalyptus grove, cinder-block privies were erected.

To rousing chanteys from the Disney era Ward's crews erected a guard fence around the cliff road and cleared a parking area atop the saddleback. In two weeks, the grounds were almost ready for rehearsals when Ward undertook a landscaping project that some of the girls referred to as a W.P.A. boondoggle.

As a Ranger captain in World War II, Ward had learned to study terrain for features disadvantageous to an enemy, and of late he had been thinking in military terms.

Westward from where the entrance road cut north, Lost Indian Canyon veered west, paralleling the saddleback, until it dwindled into a ravine west of Satan's Summit. Two hundred yards east of the summit, a huge oak, protected from fires by boulders around it and gnarled by prevailing winds, stood on a knoll overlooking the canyon. The knoll where the trees stood had been undercut by a wash eastward which fed into the canyon through a narrow defile.

At this point the canyon bent south, widening, and the view overlooked a sweep of jumbled mountains and beyond to the slate-gray Pacific. The crevice where the feeder wash looped around the knoll was shaded at the mouth by an extended limb of the oak.

Ward selected a work gang and put it to cutting, grading, and graveling a footpath four feet wide from the ranch house up and over the sadddleback, through scrub oaks and boulders. Following the draw, the path looped around the knoll and broke suddenly onto the view from the defile.

As the girls widened and graded the crevice and erected a restraining rail at the scenic viewpoint, Ward clambered around the canyon side of the knoll, unearthed a rounded boulder, and rolled it over to deeper shade under the tree, where he sat to contemplate the view and to consider his plans.

He knew his tactical planning was good, but he was concerned at the moment with his final strategy. He had to ask a favor of Diana which would involve an apparent outlay of cash, and he considered approaches. An appeal to her affection he weighed briefly and dropped. Although she wasn't too accomplished in profane love, she had no capacity whatsoever for sacred love. Thinking back over her conversations, he recalled a touch of paranoia in her make-up.

Without malice, Ward made a policy decision. Using her paranoia, he would trigger her avarice into an attack on his integrity, then counter-attack with indignation.

Three days before Labor Day, near midnight, Ward and Diana sat in her office drawing up plans for the dress rehearsal. To spare Ward's modesty, she had decided there would be no nudity on the third, or Bach, procession, since he, as sound engineer, would be present at the dress rehearsal. Her concern for his modesty, a cover for jealousy, turned him off, and he decided to deliver his ultimatum.

"As sound engineer, I'll be conspicuous in a business suit. There'll be narcotics agents in the crowd. If I'm picked up for your murder, you might be arraigned for harboring a fugitive. I recommend you buy yourself a pink suede shirt and dark glasses for me to wear at the festival."

"Write your requisition."

"Another problem's crowd control. Some of the rejuves have been isolated so long they're in no mood for coyness, and if the males make advances . . ."

"If you're suggesting I hire more guards, forget it."

"Say it's more an investment in music appreciation," he continued. "If they riot during Brahms . . ."

"I'll continue to play according to schedule."

"With no one listening. Are you sacrificing Beethoven, Brahms, and Bach to Beelzebub, Baal, and Bacchus?"

She was shamed but determined. "The primary purpose of the experiment is to test male reaction to experienced beauty and youth in the presence of inexperienced beauty and youth."

"So much for culture," he shrugged. "But I have professional pride, and as your sound engineer I couldn't perform under conditions I foresee. As your program director, I couldn't control an unrehearsed orgy."

"What do you suggest?"

"That you hire a motorcycle club, the Orange County Patriots, to police the crowd."

"I've heard of them," she nodded. "True Americans. What do you propose to pay them?"

Her question resembled a clause in an insurance policy —was the "you" generic or specific?

"Some nominal sum," he said. "Say, fifty dollars apiece."

"Do you call fifty dollars a nominal sum? How many are there?"

"Twelve or fourteen."

"No deal. That's six or seven hundred dollars out of my gate receipts."

"Our gate receipts," he reminded her.

"Don't overvalue your contributions," she snapped. "I can hire another sound engineer for less than two hundred dollars."

So she had set his pro rata at .002 of gate receipts.

Ward triggered her paranoia.

"Another sound engineer might have problems. The amplifiers haven't been connected. Eight electricians, working overtime at fifteen dollars an hour, might trace the conduits between now and Labor Day."

As he had foreseen, she wriggled easily off that hook, and then she gaffed herself.

"I'll buy a gas-driven generator, so you can write off your little conspiracy to take over the company."

"Are you accusing me of piracy?" he asked.

"Precisely."

"Very well, since you have no trust in me, I have no alternative to resignation." He arose as he spoke. "Tonight I'll sleep in the garage room, tomorrow I'll complete the wiring and return to Palo Alto. Even as a fugitive I can get a better deal from Carrick for my formula, and he already has the international organization."

"You forget, Mr. Alexander, that half the formula is mine."

"You keep your half. Carrick and I can buy enzymes by the barrel from any nursery supply house."

Fury in her eyes was replaced by avarice, which yielded to cunning, which softened into feminine loveliness, a transformation Ward recognized as a progression of affinities, before she said, "Sit down, Alex. I'm merely trying to teach a theorist how to negotiate. Of course you can have your motorcycle club. How do you contact the Patriots?"

"I couldn't," he said. "Miss Frost can."

Smiling, Diana lifted the direct line. "Miss Frost, my program director suggested I retain the Orange County Patriots to maintain crowd discipline at the love festival . . . Who's Dolores?"

Little Mama was back on the premises, now that he was gone, and contact would be made. Ward's thoughts turned to Dolores.

Somehow, he would have to cut Dolores away from the herd to work her over without interference from her bodyguard. Without injuring her seriously enough to delay his schedule, he still must produce from her screams of an intensity that would carry at least thirty yards above the Brahms *Fourth* and a massed chorus of wolf whistles.

Cupping her hand over the mouthpiece, Diana asked, "What time should they report, dear?"

Ward considered for a moment. By noon, he should have assessed punitive damages from Freddie.

"Around midday," he said. "The guard will direct them to their official parking racks, and Mr. Alexander will give them written instructions regarding procedures."

Before he finished his answer to her, Ward had hit on a method of cutting Little Mama from the herd. The Patriot closest to her would be at the yoke of the peace symbol Y, fifty yards downhill and in the crowd. If he couldn't outrun the man to the girls' privy, he deserved to forfeit a crotch job.

"You theorist," Diana chided him when she hung up. "Miss Frost predicts they'll come for ten dollars apiece."

"Good," he smiled. "But your public relations man has suggested to your grounds supervisor that a canopied throne be erected on a carpeted platform ten yards above the upper circumference of the peace symbol circle to seat a Queen of the Malibu Love Festival, to be elected by popular acclamation."

Late Sunday afternoon, September 5, Ward went alone to the oak knoll, taking a truck tire, a length of heavy rope, and a tightly capped bottle of gasoline wrapped in a T-shirt. He laid the bottle of gasoline among the boulders and swung the tire from the massive center trunk of the tree. After removing the guard rail, he could get a running start down the gravel path and launch himself, dangling by his shoulder from the tire, far out over the chasm to swing safely back onto the rocky knoll on the far side of the oak.

Finally he swung back onto the gravel path, hooking the rope over a protuberance on the east-running limb of the oak, and dangled the tire over the path. With a discus swing, he hurled the guard rail beyond the bushes and slope of the canyon wall to the bottom, forty feet below.

Walking back to the ranch house, Ward heard the girls singing as they marched up from their last rehearsal. In the pink sunset, their song filled him with peace and a warm nostalgia. They were singing an old Army song, "Violet Time," and their voices rang in lark notes over the meadows of Malibu.

Labor Day dawned bright and clear from a mild Santa

Ana breeze rolling in from the high deserts, a wonderful day for brush fires.

After a leisurely breakfast alone, Diana had to leave early for last-minute inspection of costumes. Ward signed a check on his Western Avenue bank to Freddie for one dollar. To the check he stapled his final statement:

```
For musical services rendered ............ $500.00
Less agency commission ...............    50.00
                                         ────────
                                          450.00
Less overcharge for room, board and serv-
ices previously billed to Miss Frost ......  449.00
                                         ────────
                                         $  1.00
```

Ward put the check and the statement in an envelope which he tucked into a gray suit in his wardrobe, then took all his documents relating to Albert Atascadero below and put them in the side bag of his motorcycle.

At nine, dressed in a dark blue business suit, wearing his auburn wig and dark glasses, Ward went down to the shell, carrying a typed roll of orders for the Patriots and a list of songs for Freddie. If he got past the first crucial moments with the High Wheeler, Ward knew he would not be recognized, for he planned to project an image that would completely mislead Freddie.

He intended to assess punitive damages as well as financial; in Ward's continuing dialogue with the young, it was imperative that Freddie be taught that honesty was the best policy, at least until one learned to cover his tracks.

Mustangs, dune buggies, hot rods, and Karmen Ghias of the pushers were already trickling into the parking lot. A few dealers were standing around before the shell. From the Daisy Chain, Ward recognized Won Lee, né Manuel Sanchez, from his Chinese robe. Lee was a connection and he was discussing the market with Henry Green, a dealer in imported gage, bedecked in a bright green dashiki beneath his green-dyed Afro. Little Mama knew them all and she would finger them for the Patriots, who would thus gain a monopoly on the festival trade.

Promptly at 9:30 Freddie's lavender Cadillac nosed

over the crest and stopped in the parking lot. At the distance, almost half a mile, the bass fiddle on Freddie's back resembled a bale of cotton, but in ten minutes Freddie and his two fellow members of the Untannables were breaking out of the trees and swinging over the greensward to where Ward waited.on the stage of the shell.

Ward didn't wait for them to get within speaking distance before he was shouting, "Where are the banjos? You have no banjos! Which of you is Freddie?"

"Here, sir."

"Mr. Alexander, here . . . You're supposed to play early American traditional music, minstrel songs, and spirituals."

"But, Mr. Ward said . . ."

"Mr. Ward! Mr. Ward! Where that gigolo of Miss Frost digs up you cheapies for a thousand bucks a show I'll never know. Did he tell you to submit a repertoire?"

"Yes, sir." Clambering onto the stage, Freddie extended a hand-lettered list of songs; "Feeling Groovy," "Hound Dog," "Snow Bird" . . . Ward glanced at the list, obvious distaste approaching near-apoplexy.

"This is all wrong. The theme of the festival is the development of rock, and you're to represent its crude beginnings. Your repertoire wasn't supposed to infringe on the dialectics of rock harmonics. You dig me?"

"Yes, sir."

"I figured Ward for a botch, so I prepared a list. Run through these thirty songs and select fifteen you can play." Ward handed him his list. "You'll notice the list runs pretty heavily to spirituals to show the historical development of soul. But the arrangements are up to you, understand?"

"Yes, sir."

"You can take an old favorite, say, 'Massa's in de Cold, Cold Ground,' and give it the warm McKuen touch. Here, 'Birmingham Jail' would predict the Gollenberger and Stein format to show the development of protest songs . . . You could solo 'Swing Low, Sweet Chariot' on the cello, using three strings, with a random plunk on the bass in the manner of that great artist Glamorgan."

In a staccato voice, he shot suggestions and admonitions to the trio, with Freddie listening and nodding his head. Ward ended the tirade on an order.

"Gentlemen, I must hear 'Sweet Afton,' first, and make me hear the Scottish burr and smell the heather. I have this thing about Scottish girls."

Waiting for "Sweet Afton," Ward stood on the greensward listening to the struggle on the stage, shaking his head occasionally or kicking the grass in disgust, as the trio pooled its knowledge to recall the notes of the tune. When they began, Ward listened to the first four bars.

Holding up one hand for silence, clutching his hair with the other, he ran onto the stage crying, "No, no. On the fourth measure, Freddie, just before the coda, give me an interval of glissando on a subdominant chord."

"Like this, sir?"

Freddie fingered the frets and strummed a riffle that deftly excluded the bass string. For all Ward knew, it was a perfect glissando on a subdominant chord, but he was shouting.

"No. No. No. That's African soul. I want Scottish soul. Give me more burr in that diminuendo, not a Glasgow staccato but an Edinburgh lilt. I'll stand right here until I smell the heather."

After fifteen glissandos, Ward still couldn't smell the heather.

"Listen, fellows," Ward feigned desperation, "maybe I can help the tempo by alternating the volume on the amplifiers. Take the earphones, Freddie, and I'll try to talk you into a synchronic pattern from the sound control booth."

From the air-conditioned control booth, Ward continued the harassment, his disgust mounting as the amplifiers sent the sounds caterwauling over the grounds. Before the stage, the pushers were backing off, getting closer to the grove, but the amplifiers hedged them in.

"Look, Freddie," Ward finally conceded. "Maybe Scottish evades you. Try a little African Scottish, a burr with a boogie-woogie beat . . ."

As Ward spoke, his earphones picked up a distant roar, growing in volume, becoming a rumble, which cast a terrifying double image onto his memory. Crouched in a snowy foxhole, he had heard the sound, before, in the Forest of Ardennes when the Tiger tanks of a German Panzer division had rolled toward his position.

"Hold it, Freddie."

A glance toward the skyline reassured him. Only a trickling vanguard of music lovers were coming over the ridge. Reassured, he turned back to his sound equipment, but the rumble was growing. He cast another glance toward the ridge.

Over the saddleback a motorcycle appeared, then another, and another, moving slowly in ceremonial procession. The long black line was snaking over the crest and down the approach road. Chilled by apprehension, Ward watched, counting, as the line swung toward the eucalyptus grove, fourteen Patriots dressed in black. In the lead he saw Big Papa stroking his huge Schweinjaeger, and on the seat behind him, her platinum hair flowing from beneath the azure of Ward's crash helmet, sat Little Mama.

Two hours ahead of schedule the Patriots had arrived, and the sound of their coming shook the hills. Coming early to stake out their claims to the pot trade.

Ward felt the anxiety of a man helplessly wounded as a python slithered toward him when the head of the line coiled out of the eucalyptus grove and swung south. Following instructions from the guard the Patriots would swing around and park at the ceremonial racks set fifteen yards below the privies and above the throne of the Queen of the Malibu Love Festival.

Diana's orders detailing guard procedure for the Brahms and Beethoven promenades were in the desk before him, but it would take courage to walk up the hill and hand the orders to Big Papa.

Forcing a casual tone, Ward said into the phone, "Freddie, you'd better go back to your original repertoire. I'll turn off the amplifiers so you can practice without being too conspicuous, but never again, please. No more music. The fire next time."

Ward reached into the drawer before him and pulled out the official scroll, but his eyes were on the Patriots, circling now on the final leg of their entrance. In goggles with black helmets, black jackets, black boots, all they needed was a death's-head insignia on their lapels and Ward's conditioned fear of Nazi storm troopers might have overwhelmed him. But they had forgone the straw that might have broken his will to fight. Instead, they wore tiny decals of the American flag on their dress helmets.

With orders in his hand, Ward left the booth and walked across the stage, as marked by his Establishment dress as they by their uniforms. Warning himself against the truncated stride that might have betrayed him as the pussyfooter, he moved with the easy nonchalance of a Central Avenue black on Saturday night.

Above him the line was moving behind the racks, peeling off one at a time, and Big Papa was already parking in the position of honor at the far right of the line. At eighty yards the maximum leader looked formidable to the man who walked down the steps and up the graveled walk of the peace symbol toward the dismounting line of Patriots.

Only Little Mama had seen him in full light, Ward remembered, and she had been high. The Barber knew in detail the shape of his head, but the Barber's lambency had flickered so swiftly over his skull that he doubted if the Barber could recognize it again without a phrenology chart. Still, he was twice vulnerable and as he ascended toward the line of men waiting impassively by their motorcycles, dark blue star-spangled billy clubs hanging from their belts, he felt again his old Normandy Landing Syndrome, the tongue-fuzzing dryness of mouth, the kidney pressure, the keying of fear to resolution.

To Ward's left stood the officers, gold stars gleaming above their jacket pockets. Brazos was the two-star, now, but Arms, not the Barber, was the new one-star. The Barber stood in the ranks, next to Arms. Apparently he had suffered the fate of experts in any bureaucracy. He was too gifted to be promoted.

Now images from his memory, triggered by the line of troops, came to Ward's aid. Once more he was a Ranger captain commencing inspection. Unconsciously his musculature made adjustments. He drew in his stomach, squared his shoulders, set his face in officious lines, and contracted his sphincter. Fifty yards from the troopers and inwardly counting cadence, Ward stepped smartly from the yoke of the peace symbol doing a right oblique away from the leader's end of the column. His military pace alerted the Patriots and he caught a visible stiffening, a surreptitious dressing to the right.

Striding directly toward the left pivot man, a lard-bottomed Patriot with the hip spread of a female, Ward found him repugnant before he got within nose shot. The man's eyes were blue gimlets buried in a ball of dough from which jutted a thin, aristocratic nose as out of place on the face as a yacht's prow on a garbage scow. Sweat oozing from his fat streaked the dirt on his skin, making him look greasier than the oil-splattered motorcycle he stood beside. A blond fuzz which could have been removed with one swipe of a depilatory grew above his lip. Ward had seen mustaches grown with more authority by old maids.

Stenciled in flaking yellow above the pocket of the Patriot's jacket Ward could read the name "No Balls," and suddenly he was fighting to conceal his astonishment. These thirteen bulls and one heifer were letting a steer run with their herd. Ward's kick had done it. The toe he had planted three months ago had borne this bloated fruit. Beneath the dewlap jowls and flatulence of No Balls were hidden the once patrician form and features of the two-star, Ball Bearing.

Down the column Ward walked, slapping the rolled orders against his thigh in the manner of a British officer with a swagger stick. Slowly his eyes traveled from top to bottom of each Patriot and flicked a glance at each machine. They were all there, Sprocket, Razor, Hoot Owl, the Loon, Lefty, Muffler, Breeches, Drain Oil, Crotch Job, the Barber, Arms, and Brazos, and then Ward came face to face with Big Papa.

Face to face but not front to front. Big Papa had taken a step forward, swiveling on his hips with his left thigh foremost, guarding his crotch. Ward halted before the barrier but his eyes continued their inspection of Little

Mama. She wouldn't recognize him. The bemused smile and vacant eyes beneath his crash helmet told him that. Dolores was flying so high she needed an oxygen mask. But for a split second Ward's gaze lingered on the pneumatic outthrust of her breasts.

Then he was clicking his heels and handing Big Papa the scroll.

"These are your orders with the schedule for the exhibition of the groupies. Permit no spectator to pinch or stroke until the promenade in the nude commences. Prior to the program there will be an election by acclamation of a Festival Queen, who will be seated on the throne."

Big Papa didn't unroll his orders. He handed them to Brazos, who handed them to Arms, who handed them to the Barber.

"We brought the queen with us."

"Reposing special trust and confidence in your ability to judge feminine pulchitrude, I then hereby cancel the acclamation of a queen and install your choice on the throne."

"What'd he say, Barber?"

"I don't know, Big Papa, but it sounded like a compliment."

Ward spoke to Big Papa, "Before the festivities commence, move your men among the crowd and confiscate all pot or hard stuff. When Miss Aphrodite comes on stage, clear the gravel paths and station your men according to the written procedure. Permit no premature grouping before the Bach processional. Understood?"

"You dig him, Barber?"

"Got him."

"The queen will be crowned with a golden crown during the first promenade."

"She's got her crown," Big Papa rumbled.

"Want a golden crown, Big Papa," Dolores mumbled.

"Nobody touches your head but me, Little Mama."

Big Papa was wrong, Ward thought, as he saluted, did a left face, and strode back to the shell. Little Mama would get her crown and more besides, for her world lines had once again swung Ward into her orbit. He had never felt such affinity for a female.

Propelled by pneumatic thrusts, he tripped lightly onto the stage, calling, "Back to the earphones, Freddie."

Once more in the sound control room, Ward flicked on switches, setting the amplifiers for a maximum interference, and said, "Once more to the repertoire, Freddie. Ah, one, ah, two, ah, three . . . Hit it."

But no sounds caterwauled from the amplifiers. Instead, Freddie's voice came over his earphones. "All right, Al. When are you going to quit this she-it and play ball?"

"Freddie, how'd you know it was me?"

"When you cakewalked across the stage after you left Dolores. What's this all about?"

"You've been assessed punitive damages for an overcharge on my rent and board . . So, we can knock it off, Sherlock, and I'll take you to lunch."

But Ward was talking to an embryonic lawyer.

"Where's your old man with my bread?"

"He'll be here at two-thirty."

"Make sure he is," Freddie chuckled. "Those crackers out front are looking for a blond-haired pussyfooter who owes them a crotch job."

CHAPTER TEN

Ward and the trio lunched in the east wing amid a twitter of females, and Freddie recalled his encounter with the FBI. "That Culpepper kept smelling my Aqua Velva and jerking my Afro."

After lunch, the trio returned to work and Ward went to the penthouse office, which he had to himself since Diana was assembling the rejuves for the grand march to the pavilions. He called and reserved a seat on the five o'clock flight to San Jose and then dialed Ester to arrange for her to pick him up at the airport and to permit Cabroni's wiretap to record his conversation.

Ester bubbled with the latest news. She had flown to Stockholm, where she had "wired" him into the Nobel Committee. Carrick dropped by occasionally to see her and to talk over his problem. He had approved Ward's request for a lower research grant, which Ward had expected, but Carrick's problem interested him more because it seemed similar to Diana's. "His psychiatrist says he doesn't want to make love or war," Ester said. "He wants to make money."

Finally she asked, "How's Mexico?"

"I'm on my way home, but I'm dropping by Ruth Gordon's Adorable U Beauty Ranch, at 2:30, just to say hello."

"You're supposed to have done away with her," Ester said accusingly.

"In a way I have," he assured her, knowing Ester and Cabroni would read different meanings in his remark, "but I'll be at the San Jose airport at six. Can you meet me?"

"Love to. I've been longing for a little domestic peace ever since you left. But, darling, don't get any more underwear. I found a deal on boxer shorts and bought you two dozen pairs."

So she had brushed off Cabroni and gotten a body-guard in the bargain. Clever woman, Ester, Ward thought, as he hung up.

And he couldn't find a better wife, as his recent experiences had taught him. Any husband who stepped out on his wife was a fool for compounding his original error.

His call should get Cabroni to the ranch by 2:30.

Ward showered and shaved for the second time today, carefully combed his wavy blond hair, buffed his finger-nails, and put on his denim jeans, the pink suede shirt, and his boots.

At ten minutes to one, he laid out his gray suit, shirt, matching tie and socks, and a pair of shoes. Regardless of his presence or absence, Diana's horological ethics would hold her to the programmed schedule, and he didn't wish to make an appearance on the grounds until ten minutes into the Brahms *Fourth*. His experiment was scheduled to start a little later than Diana's.

Ward took his auburn wig below and stuffed it into the side bag of his motorcycle with the Atascadero iden-tification papers. From the store room he removed the papier-mâché queen's crown and six inches of dynamite fuze he had salvaged from a blasting project. He lashed the crown to the fender rack and taped the fuze to the top of the gas tank of the motorcycle, inserting one end into a percussion cap which he stuck inside the gasoline tank.

Clearly revealed as the boy who, in trust and friend-ship, had first pussyfooted into the parking lot of the Daisy Chain, Ward rolled his machine onto the parking lot, jumped astride it, and coasted down the approach road to the bend where he swung into the grove, follow-ing his plotted path which exited behind the restroom. Below he could hear Brahms, played with Diana's metro-nomic skill, rising over wolf calls and whistles. From re-hearsals, Ward could tell by the music he had almost five minutes before the advent of the forties.

Crouching low with Little Mama's crown, he parked behind the restroom and sprinted to the line of Patriot motorcycles, where he paused to scout downslope. Through a bright golden haze over the meadow, he saw the two lines of Grecian shepherdesses, flinging poppies left and right, had split at the yoke of the Y and were moving toward the perimeter of the circle. All Patriots were on station, pacing back and forth inside the restraining ropes, their star-spangled clubs at the ready.

A shirtless boy slipped under the rope as Ward watched and made a lunge at a blonde thirty-eight, but before a finger could touch a thigh, Sprocket, patrolling the area, moved with the speed of a riot policeman to club the youth to the ground. The whomp of the club could be heard by Ward. Waddling over at top speed, No Balls dragged the body off the path.

Hypnotized by the parade, few spectators noticed the clubbing or another by the Owl on the opposite extender of the Y. Two spectators leaped at the same rejuve in Arms territory and were dispatched with a zap-zap. Then Brazos got three and Ward distinctly saw the sadist, Barber, club a youth who merely leaned too far over the ropes.

The lines of nymphs were beginning to weave around the obstructions. Big Papa had made an error by assigning only No Balls to the clean-up detail. Bodies were accumulating faster than the eunuch could drag them from the path.

But Ward could not be too critical of Big Papa's planning when suddenly faced with an error of his own. The forties began to emerge from the tents, throwing their poppies in the style of shot putters and the quantum jump in the crowd noise was much greater than the arithmetic progression between breast sizes. Hooees, wolf yells, and whistles threatened to drown out Brahms. On the one hand, Ward wondered hopefully whether the sound signified that his obsession was the common lot of males, and on the other he was sickened by apprehension. The noise could destroy his plans by raising the decible level higher than any he might generate from Dolores.

Now was the moment, and the moment might have come too late.

Ward stepped before the throne and leaned near the

ear of the bemused queen gazing on her subjects below. "Coronation time. Come, Little Mama, and get your golden crown."

He backed away from her, standing with his heels almost to the edge of the dais, and held high her crown, its gilt gleaming and its glass rubies and emeralds glittering in the filtered sunlight.

Without removing Ward's helmet, regal in her euphoria, Dolores rose from the throne, her breasts heaving as if her lungs were there. She saw the blond hair, the pink suede shirt, and desire in his gray eyes. Her lips formed a phrase he read, "BMW 280 . . .Wow."

Then she was floating toward him, her arms spread for a lover's embrace, her smile dimpling, and Ward's resolution wavered. In trust and in the joy of reunion, she came to him, and in an innocence that left her crotch unguarded. His nature revolted against the rejection of any woman offering the ultimate gift of womanhood, but coldly planned policy and the noises below demanded that he kick the gift-bearer in the gift.

Patriotism found the spur to his weakening resolve. The decal of Old Glory, still adhering to his azure helmet, was scratched and dirty. His left leg tensed. His right leg pivoted free.

Dolores was drifting closer.

Suddenly an insight struck him. A ritual kick should be sufficient; a fillip of contempt for her femininity would spare his chivalry, strike a blow for country, and rid him, symbolically at least, of breast obsessions. His offense to the girl's ego would release a scream of indignation loud enough to draw attention to his deed.

With a swift but soft uncoiling Ward's leg stroked out and up. His toe, held rigid, landed as lightly as a dove in a dovecote.

Instinctively the girl clamped her thighs, but his boot was there, and her unaccustomed action threw her backward, screaming, as Ward was catapulted forward. The crown went tumbling as he threw out his arms to break his fall. Chest over breasts, they fell, and Ward bounced upward to his feet again, rebounding from a resilience suspiciously like that of silicone, to barely escape her embrace.

Dolores's continuing screams were squeals of delight. Though free to flee, Ward held his position out of chivalry and from expediency. Arching over her mammoth heavings, Dolores's squeals keened unnoticed to the crowd below. A few spectators on the upper fringes did, indeed, look back, but only in passing wonder at such a strange hang-up to have in one's bag. From the sounds, it was easy for the viewers to assume that he and Dolores were merely doing their thing.

In a sense, Ward knew they were correct. Looking backwards, prancing in mark time, he knew he was hooked in a figurative sense, and her breasts had done it.

Then, that which had almost destroyed Ward's plans saved them.

When E-44 emerged from the pavilion, a silence of awe and reverence fell over the multitude. Between the notes of Brahms, the shrieked urgings of Little Mama were clearly audible. "Faster, Little Papa. Faster."

. Suddenly the cry of the Loon quavered over the crowd, "That pinko's back, Big Papa, and he's pussyfooting Little Mama."

The alarm from the Patriots' lookout was Ward's cue for an exit, but gallantry bade him stay.

"Brazos, Arms, front and center." Rage lifted Big Papa's voice into thunder. "Crotch Job, man your chains."

The last bone-chilling order freed Ward from all claims of gallantry. This was no time for pussyfooting. Ward bounded toward the girls' john with Little Mama's plea trailing him.

"Come back, Little Papa."

Well, inconstancy was the better part of romance, Ward thought, leaping into the saddle, but to two things men were constant ever.

He gunned the BMW 280 from behind the washroom and throttled down, describing a series of slow figure-eights below the margin of the trees. Watching, he saw the Patriots detaching themselves unhurriedly from the crowd, and he knew the patterns he wove with his motor-

cycle had slowed their haste. Prior research done unobtrusively along the Sunset Strip had explained the patterns. His figure-eights were a challenge to a game of hare
and hounds.

Conventions of the contest were rigid. The chase did
not begin until the leader of the hounds dropped his arm,
and wherever the hare led, the hounds must follow on
pain of being branded "chicken."

Twenty yards below Ward, the Patriots sauntered
toward their machines. Farther below, two lines of shepherdesses wound unnoticed along gravel paths, tossing
poppies to a crowd that had turned to look up the slope.
Farthest below, the tiny figure of Diana bent over her
piano, oblivious to all save her schedule and the metro-
nome beating in her head.

"He'p me with my ballast, Arms," Papa called.

Arms came and the two men lifted Little Mama, limp
from speed and satiety, to the rear seat of the Schweinjaeger and strapped her where she lolled, dream-lost and
smiling.

All Patriots stood beside their hogs, now, facing toward
Ward as they pulled on goggles and gauntlets and cinched
the straps of their crash helmets. They faced Ward but
did not look at him, in a dismissal both contemptuous and
Calvinistic, as if his fate were settled, preordained, and
no power of the law or social agencies could prevent or
even delay the inevitable crotch job.

"Patriots, start your engines!" Big Papa's order rolled
down the line and the sound of motors shivered the now
purple haze over the meadow.

Big Papa's arm was raised as he glanced down the
line and Ward, on the downslope of the segment of a
circle, was watching the arm. Ward timed his start
perfectly. As he swung into an upslope segment of his
weave, looking over his shoulder he saw the arm drop.

The chase was on.

As if scorning suicide Ward gunned his BMW 280
straight toward the trees, splitting a distance between
two eucalyptuses so narrow that scales from both trunks
were brushed away by his Levis. Swerving among the

boles, dipping below projections, along a course he had rehearsed for weeks, he cleared tiny gullies over concealed embankments and arched over protruding roots on inconspicuous stone bridges. Leaves shook from the sound of his passing, but the roar behind him diminished.

Angling into the approach road on the bight of its southward bend, he gunned toward the ranch house at ninety, slowing as he neared the parking area and skewing to a halt where the footpath to Lover's Leap commenced.

Ostensibly as a gesture of contempt, Ward, who hadn't smoked since the Surgeon General's Report, paused and lit a cigarette as he waited for the hounds to clear the trees.

Big Papa's powerful and ballasted Schweinjaeger broke first from the grove, its driver looking right and left until he spotted prey up the slope.

"Rabbit, one o'clock high!" he yelled as other Patriots emerged onto the road.

Ward took a deep draw from his cigarette, touched it to the fuze on his gas tank, and flipped it downhill as he straddle-walked his vehicle onto the hikers' trail and started in "low."

The hounds, plus bitch, could not head him off at the pass because the field between was clustered with boulders and dense with chaparral. They had to follow him.

Ward drove slowly along the winding gravel lane. Behind, he heard Big Papa cut in his supercharger and he knew the entire pack had cleared the woods. He glanced back and saw them hit the gravel at a full seventy, driving with superb skill, as he, using the broken-wing technique of a quail, pretended to pick his way along the lane.

Keeping an eye on them in his rear view mirror, he drove with one hand, loosening the cap on his gas tank and losing another twenty yards in the maneuver. When the leader was a mere thirty yards behind, Ward, in apparent panic, gunned his vehicle forward and hit the banking turn into the feeder ravine at fifty. Out of sight, he coasted, braking to forty for the curving run to the precipice. This speed for this curve at this banking angle had been calculated beforehand. Balancing his machine, he prepared for the trick he could not rehearse.

He hit the straightaway and threw his feet to the handlebars, guiding with his heels and balancing atop the seat. Ahead, eight feet from the ledge, the truck tire dangled from the knob of the overhanging limb and the opening in the tire seemed no larger than a pinhole as he aimed his right forearm at the aperture and the motorcycle hurtled toward the precipice.

Braced for an arm-wrenching tug, a shoulder separation, or even death in a possible fall, he jabbed his right arm through the tire and clamped his left hand around his wrist. The rope had slack enough to permit him to run straight before swinging into the arc of the rope and the tire's resilience absorbed the shock.

Ward rode his Molotov cocktail over the precipice, but as the machine dropped to the canyon floor to splatter into a mounting ring of fire he was making a lazy half-circle in the sky. On the far side of the oak knoll, he landed on his prepared spot with less shock than he remembered as a parachutist at the Arnheim Drop.

Holding his tire in the crook of his arm, he watched the mouth of the feeder ravine.

Whoosh!

Big Papa came first. His shaft-driven Schweinjaeger shot from the ledge to plummet into the chasm, Little Mama clinging behind. Her platinum hair, flying from under Ward's azure helmet, reminded him of the wings of a butterfly, fluttering high. Before Big Papa whomped into the brush and rocks below, Arms and Brazos, following, were airborne above their maximum leader. Then in order they came: the Barber, Breeches, Crotch Job, Drain Oil, Lefty, the Loon, Muffler, the Owl, Razor, Sprocket, No Balls, and an unidentified fellow traveler on a green Triumph.

Some fell with receding screams of terror terminated by the crunch of crushed metal, but the last crunch did not end in silence.

From forty feet above, Ward heard the *harrooom* of runaway motors, the wham and whoosh of exploding gasoline tanks, an occasional scream from a reviving survivor, and the crackle of burning brush. He marveled at the adaptability of nature. Chaparral was a scrub conditioned by fire; it burned quickly and it was germinated by flames which broke open its seed pods.

With the additional gasoline spraying the canyon walls, Ward doubted if he would have to use his conventional Molotov cocktail cached earlier, until he noticed that the rotundity of Arms had let his body roll down the canyon, clear of the flames which were mounting the draw. Arms sat looking groggily at a broken forearm dangling from the elbow he held before him. If Arms revived enough in time to act, he could escape down the canyon.

Ward rolled the T-shirt, inserted it into the bottle, let it saturate, lighted it, and hurled the fire bomb. Smoke from its wick scrawled a a crude series of O's through the air, such as those from a child's penmanship exercise, as the bottle arced down the ravine to explode ten yards below the befuddled Arms and ensure him an invitation to the Patriots' barbecue.

Looking down on the holocaust, Ward realized the scene would appear gruesome to anyone, other than a Vietnam veteran, who lacked scientific objectivity, but Ward was a veteran of the Dachau, Buchenwald, Bergen-Belsen generation and this was merely a warm-up for another scene he was dreading to watch.

Because he was a war veteran and a scientist Ward was almost shocked by an improbability.

As the growl of motors diminished under the crackle of flames, a figure emerged from the pit, climbing hand over hand and dragging a maimed leg behind, grasping at shrubbery, roots, projecting rocks, finding handholds where none should have been. Incredibly, the man was keeping ahead of the fire line. As he climbed upward, Ward recognized behind the dirt and blood the face of the Barber, whose arms apparently held superhuman strength as well as artistry. Even granting that the fire gave him extra impetus, Ward felt the struggle was a tribute to the young man's survival instinct. The Barber was a sadist, but he was tough.

As he climbed nearer, Ward heard him crying, "Hellup,

hellup," with a hoarse yelping quality to his voice which gave Ward pause until he identified the correlative sound —the barking of a seal.

Ward had provided for such a contingency. He hoisted the boulder he had placed under the oak—it was almost as large and fully as round as the Tom Watson watermelons grown on his father's farm—and set it nearer the edge of the precipice. For a moment he studied the lie of the boulder. The Barber was climbing fifteen yards beneath an overhang which obstructed the roll, but there was another obstruction to the right and below the overhang protecting the climber.

Ward moved the boulder approximately fourteen centimeters to the right of its original location and waited a moment for the Barber's climb to bring him to an invisible X Ward drew on the cliff face. Then he shoved the boulder off the ledge.

As he had calculated, the granite ball caromed off the right ledge and dropped toward the Barber. The Barber's mouth was open to bellow "Help" when the boulder scored a perfect strike on his head, strangling the cry with his teeth and collapsing jawbone. Probably his mandible was driven into his tonsils, but the force of the blow became an academic consideration when the Barber fell backward to join his fellow members of the Orange County Patriots' Motorcycle Club and Self-Immolation Society.

Ward stood for a moment brushing the dirt off his hands and studying the flames. Confined as it was within the walls of the ravine, the fire could have been extinguished at the moment by a single borate bomber, but it would be an hour before such measure could be taken.

Ordinarily, Ward detested the fad words of the intelligentsia. Next to "dialogue," used without reference to the dramatic arts, he disliked the current vogue for "eschatology," used outside church ritual. Looking down, he felt no regret for the mass suicides; rather, a satisfying awareness of final things, the emotions of eschatology in their true sense.

Not one of those boys could have made it alone in a competitive economy; they simply were not Establishment material. The only immediate meaning their deaths held for society would not be apparent until the winter rains came to the re-seeded watershed. Above their charred calcium, the tufts of rye grass might grow a little greener.

Ecologically, Ward felt an abiding sense of accomplishment. Weighed non-contemporaneously, these deaths would benefit all successive generations. A source of pollution had been removed from the flow of evolution.

Remembering a line from Euripides, Ward quoted it aloud as a requiescat for the Patriots, "Of strong things find you not any as strong as the strings of fate."

Those below had eaten of the lotus of violence and each had been foredoomed by his short time-horizon. They had lived on the perilous edge and had dropped over the edge, together. Once each had had a separate rendezvous with death, at midnight on some flaming mattress, at some highway patrol's disputed barricade; a few would have ended as greasy periods below exclamation points drawn on concrete in burnt rubber. Now Ward, their *deus ex machismo*, had twisted the strings of their fate into a single knot of brotherhood eternal.

Standing there, where the mountains look on Malibu and Malibu looks on the sea, he felt, finally, the catharsis of a Prometheus, chthonian yet Olympian, who had stolen from the gods not the gift of fire but of death. His dialogue with this segment of the young was complete. They had learned by example always to do unto others before it was done unto them.

Now, to the festival and the continuing dialogue.

Ward took off his shirt, weighted it with his boots, and hurled the evidence that connected him with the Patriots onto the pyre. He hated to lose the shirt, an eighty-dollar item, but the boots were ruined. If he wore them around Palo Alto, every cat in the neighborhood would be trailing behind him.

In barefeet and T-shirt, Ward jogged back to the ranch house. In the twenty-five minutes before Gollenberger and Stein were to play he had to dress and make three anonymous calls to report his location to the LAPD, the FBI, and the L.A. County Sheriff's Office. To be fair and to create jurisdictional confusion, he wanted all departments on the scene with Joe Cabroni as a witness who could recognize Ruth Gordon. Now, as a civic duty, he would also have to report the fire, before he ripped the veil from the face of Medusa and revealed her attendant Gorgons.

When Ward reached the eucalyptus grove on his return to the meadow, he knew Diana had established the competitive factor in her experiment beyond doubt.

Drifting up through the trees, hollow-eyed from shock, dazed, some weeping, a horde of young people were making their way toward the parking lot. Ward had seen such expressions among civilian evacuees of war-shattered towns in Europe, and as of old he cloaked his mind with a soldier's apathy. But his cloak was tattered from long disuse and it took an effort of will to count a random sample of the émigrés, twenty girls and two boys. One of the boys was being drawn, almost forcibly, by a girl, possibly his older sister, so Ward was somewhat uncertain that his sampling was accurate.

They had a right to be shocked. They were the walking wounded from point zero of a biological nuclear explosion. He wanted to shout, "Forget it, girls. This bomb will be defuzed."

But they would not forget. In her own continuing dialogue with the young, Diana had convinced them, with utter finality, they should never trust anyone, over or under thirty.

On the other hand, they would not talk, and the experiment would never reach the record books of science for other biologists to attempt.

To the final movement of Bach's *Passion*, Ward emerged from the eucalyptus grove dressed in Establishment style. In the distance, Diana bent over her piano in a concentration touching on the sublime, because the intervening scene made Bach's *Passion* resemble a Parcheesi game between two maiden aunts.

As Ward foresaw, the rejuves had not completed the Beethoven processional, since remnants of miniskirts were still draped around their waists, shoulder straps dangling, breakaway panties broken away. Spread below him, bodies undulated like waves on a lake. Here and there the surface boiled in a sudden frenzy as if some underground trout had risen to bite a fly. As Ward strode nearer, the general view yielded to the particular. Some of the youths slept from satiety, others sat and waited, while some more enterprising—Establishment material—stood and looked around for the flurry of activity which indicated the impending availability of a rejuve.

Moving among them, now, very carefully, listening to the low moans of lewd females, Ward realized the scene might appear shocking to anyone who had never seen an X-rated movie. On the other hand, some inveterate habitués of the stroke houses might find reason to be critical—the bodies weren't aligned at good camera angles. But at the moment Ward was less concerned with cinematic verities than with his shoes; already, today, he had ruined a pair of good boots.

It was no scene for a man from the swinging years of selective love-ins, yet if the pianist from the flapper era on the stage in front of him had her way, these undulations were the wave of the future—and all for a few million bucks.

Ward was disgusted with the woman at the piano, but he had another contribution in his continuing dialogue with the young which would teach these boys that sex was a hormone-based LSD that hallucinated today's Waldorf salad from tomorrow's cold potatoes.

As he bounded up the steps, Diana was finishing the finale and Ward realized that, in her, no great artist would be lost to arthritis. Her staccatos skipped, her allegros wept, and she hung to a bar like a dipsomaniac. He could get better Bach from a player piano.

Inside the artists' dressing room, Ward found Gollenberger reading Odet's *Waiting for Lefty* and Stein reading Veblen's *The Theory of the Leisure Class*.

"Time, gentlemen." Ward spoke with authority that needed no introduction. "Give me 'Flutter High, Butterfly' with an encore, if needed. If not, I'll give you the cut signal and you can go home."

Gollenberger and Stein accepted his authority and rose to get their instruments.

Ward hurried to the control room and turned the amplifiers to maximum treble. The last five notes of Bach's *Passion* clanged over the meadow like whangs from an epicene Chinese gong.

As Gollenberger and Stein plugged in their instruments, Ward walked over to Diana. She was exhausted by her hour's ordeal, drooping on the piano bench, but she revived when he bent and kissed her neck.

"Darling, your performance was incredible," he spoke honestly. "If you never play again, you can always remember this hour."

Glowing wanly at his compliment, she flexed her hands and looked up at him. "But, dearest, you were not in the sound booth."

"I stopped by the restroom, and when I heard you playing I was transfixed," he answered truthfully.

"That's sweet of you, Alex, but your *pro rata* is predicated on your services. I'll have to dock you a percentage for being absent."

"No cost is too great for this experience. Come, and while you get rested we'll peek."

As he helped her from the stool, she asked, "Where is my beautiful auburn hair?"

Again he answered truthfully. "It got too hot for the wig."

Hand in hand they walked to the stage and gazed out over the undulations. Diana's courses in interpretive dancing were paying off. Definite classical elements were in the movements below them, Ionic merging with Doric, and here and there the opulence of Byzantine.

Clinging possessively to his arm, Diana disturbed his thought by beginning her infernal humming, throating a few bars of "Hello, Young Lovers."

"Isn't love grand?" she asked rhetorically. "Such a many-splendored thing. Really though, Alex, it's not what you do but the way that you do it."

Frankly he was getting slightly tired of her pop-titled libido and answered rather brusquely, "It's what's up front that counts."

"Now, you're being crude," she flashed, but the scene spread before them was not one to permit prolonged vexation. Obviously she was eager to get down among them, but he was done with his days of grass and roses.

"Alex," she beseeched, subliminally, "we've got syncopated rhythm. Don't you think we could teach these youngsters a thing or two?"

"They'll synchronize better with music. We'll sit here on the stage and watch pragmatism pay off. Then, when you're rested . . ."

Turning back to Gollenberger and Stein he said, "Hit it, boys."

As the first waves of "Flutter High, Butterfly" tore through them, they sat, Diana snuggling close in a liquefaction of thighs.

Arms around each other's waists, they sat and listened, watching the tempo on the grass speed up to the tempo of the music.

Suddenly she said, "You mouth the word 'pragmatism' like a preacher pronounces 'prostitution.' "

Already she was two weeks past the honeymood period, beginning to pick at trifles.

"I don't disrespect prostitution, dear. A skilled prostitute is a commercial artist."

"Love's not a financial arrangement, Alex. You sound materialistic."

Her first projection of her own defects onto her spouse, he noted. This meant she was well past the honeymoon stage, but he answered her charge with silence, and his silence disturbed her. They listened for a moment and she turned to him, contrite. "You do love me, don't you, Alex?"

Now she was seeking the reassurance so vital to an aging matron, he observed. The high notes were vibrating against her unstable molecules of reconstituted DNA. Her innercellular structure was being altered; the random errors of age were piling up.

"Whenever you want me to," he answered.

"That's not what I meant at all," she said. "After all, there's more to the relationship between a man and a woman than just sex. There's companionship."

Her years were truly winging by.

"If they both enjoy a good game of backgammon," he agreed. "I don't play backgammon."

Now she lapsed into a frigid silence which he welcomed because there were other observations he wished to make. Watching the celebrants below, he hoped the cellular structure of the rejuves held until the sustained staccato he had written into the song's finale. Out of sheer humanity, he wanted their last act to end in a soaring climax.

Also he was looking for Freddie to arrange transportation to Hollywood, where he could catch the airlines bus. When he spotted his former soul brother, he felt disgust.

Freddie had cut E-44 from the herd and was attempting a Kittibangi Crawl with an ineptness that was wrecking the image of black exoticism Ward had erected and, unknown to the High Wheeler, setting the progress of African eroticism back two generations.

Fixing the coordinates of Freddie's location in his mind, Ward shifted his gaze to a closer view. Almost below him, he saw E-24 in the arms of a towheaded lad of sixteen or seventeen. As Ward watched, Gollenberger and Stein swung into the sustained staccato. E-24's partner responded, but the little Cajun seemed stuck in gumbo mud.

"My guests are breaking rhythm," Diana complained. "They're not holding the beat."

Her voice quavered and he glanced down. Her skin was growing crepey and her eyes crepuscular. Once disintegration commenced, it progressed on a sine curve, he had calculated. Diana was swooping down the curve.

"What's happening to T-11?" she asked. "Her arms look withered."

"She's taking an awful pounding," Ward commented, "because love's a total involvement in a maximum environment."

His quote was taken from her text, but she made no comment as he looked back toward Gollenberger and Stein and gave them the "cut" sign.

"She's growing old, Alex," the beldame beside him

shrieked. "Look at her flesh . . . Where are those boys going? I'm paying them to play."

"I dismissed them, Ruth. Your voice is so weak I couldn't hear what you were saying."

"Quit calling me Ruth. Look, my guests are beginning to look repulsive."

She was breezing past fifty, now, at the point where his innercellular structure would hold.

"You're applying the aesthetics of the 'now' generation to the 'then' generation," he explained.

"But what's happening out there?"

Polite as always, Ward attempted to break the news to her gently. "Did you ever read Hawthorne's *Doctor Heidegger's Experiment*, Ruth?"

"This is no damned time for a literary discussion," she snapped, "and quit calling me Ruth."

Ward was tired, himself, slightly irritable, and he didn't like to hear a woman use profanity.

"You *are* Ruth. Look at your hands," he snapped.

She looked.

"I'm growing old!"

Horror in her voice aroused his compassion, and he turned to her gently. "One can grow beautiful with age, Ruth. So many fine things do. Old lace, old wine, Swiss cheese . . ."

"Like W-27 there?" She pointed a bony finger, her voice cracking with disgust.

She had a point, Ward admitted. It would take a complex theory of esthetics to advance an argument favoring the rejuves over the Rockettes, and the other half of his control group was becoming aware of the transfigurations. A male voice screamed from the center area, "Bad trip . . . Get my guru. I'm freaking out."

In the upper right quadrant, another boy screamed in a shriller tone, "Save me, Filmore. My Virginia's a werewolf."

But the most plaintive wail of all reached his ears from close at hand. "Grandmother, you!"

Curses, moans, pleas, religious invocations were rising from the crowd. A young theorist jumped to his feet, shouting, "It's the smoke, fellows. The pot fumes are caught in an inversion layer. We're hallucinating. Everybody keep calm and quit breathing."

Ward glanced down at E-24.

The petite and bouncy French girl, a scaled-down 46, was rising from the arms of her teenage lover, who had fainted. Her chestnut hair once glossy with highlights resembled a rag mop. The breast which had launched the only Springbok Spin of a white man had fallen, and the sight was enough to cure any but the most confirmed deviate of breast obsession.

She struggled to her feet with the strength of a woman of eighty years fast dwindling to that of the ninety-year-old who finally stood up, bent, tottering, looking around her with the dazed wonderment and helplessness of the very old. Remembering the fatigue accelerated aging had caused in him the first time, Ward felt the weariness that crushed her ancient frame. Yet, she stood there, a tiny, gallant veteran, home from the wars she now must barely remember.

Even so, remembering the charm of her accent, the grace and vitality of her youth, he could have loved her, still, as antiquarians love the Parthenon, for the glory that once had been.

Ward welcomed the distraction of approaching helicopters. Cabroni's was the northern one, he assumed, coming from the Camarillo air strip. The blue one from the west with the Navy star was definitely the ONI from Point Mugu. Two eastward were the FBI and the LAPD, and one from the south was the L.A. County Sheriff's Office. On Fiend's Crest Drive, he could hear a siren sounding louder and clearer over the subdued sounds of weeping from the meadow.

"Listen, Ruth. They're playing our song."

She had no ear for subtle humor.

"Alex, what shall I do?"

It was the first time he recalled her asking his advice. Since he was a considerate person, he considered her problem in relation to the fire, which had swept out of the canyon and was rolling down the hillside toward the ranch house.

"I suggest you hurry to your office and call in your mini-buses to get your patients back to their homes, because your ranch house will soon be burning."

"You go, Alex. I'm too tired."

Since Ward was a just man, he considered this her mess and her duty to clean it up.

"I have only enough time to arrange transportation back to Hollywood."

Above them, to the east of the grove, the helicopters bearing officials were touching down on a grassy knoll.

He was walking from the stage when a thought struck him and he turned and called back to her, "You'll soon be getting aid from local, state, and federal authorities, possibly even the CIA."

Shouldering through dazed young men and stepping around seated oldsters, Ward approached the High Wheeler, who was explaining to a member of his trio, "This is what they call group hysteria or the madness of crowds. We were just conned into thinking the old babes were chicks."

Every man here would have his own explanation figured in another ten minutes, Ward realized, as he walked up.

"Freddie, I'm Doctor Alexander Ward. Al told me you were a very accommodating and resourceful young man. He left a check for you and I'll add a little extra if you can drive me back to Hollywood in something of a hurry. We'll settle both accounts when you get there."

Remembering the news story, the High Wheeler reverted to the Hustler. "Yes, sir, Doctor Ward. You just circle around that hill there, keeping out of sight of those gentlemen by the helicopters, and slide into the back seat of the only lavender Cadillac in the parking lot. Soon as we pick up our instruments in the artists' dressing room, I'll have you to Hollywood in no time at all."

Ward ducked into the crowd, keeping low, as if heeding Freddie's advice. He did not wish to deny Freddie this last furtive pleasure.

Composed dignity would be his ploy with the authorities, Ward decided as he made his way toward Cabroni to wish him a good day. The only charge they had against him was the suspected murder of Ruth Gordon, and they were stuck with the charge.

Face-saving would be their shuffle. No officer would detain a Nobel nominee for murder in the presence of his alleged victim, alive though slightly confused, and in the presence of rival authorities. The story would not look good in the S.F. *Chronicle,* the L.A. *Times,* and the Washington *Post.* His dinner with Ester would not be delayed.

Thoughts of Ester swung Ward's mind from less immediate considerations.

At times, all of us wish to go back and follow the path not taken, he thought, to know loves brighter than loves we have known, but the same player would make the same errors in a different ball park. From his first youth he owned a graveyard in Germany and from his second a crematorium on Malibu.

Youth, he decided, was not merely a chronological condition, but a process of learning. To grow old was to become aware of one's limitations and, now, he accepted his, knowing within his limits his theoretical skills would still provide the more abundant life. One final application of the youth solution to Ester's upper torso would do it.

Backgammon and Parcheesi were not in his retirement bag.